Just

One

look

ISBN-9780995097995

ALSO BY MARIA LA SERRA

The Proverbial Mr.Universe

Lyrical Lights

The One & Only

ABOUT THE BOOK

What do a hotshot lawyer and a moonlighting beauty have in common? Not much, but when they have to put their differences aside for a good cause, anything can happen. Maybe even love.

Victoria Fairfax wasn't looking for love. Instead, she was hoping to earn enough money to start her own catering business by working nights as a bartender for charity events. However, love might have been looking for her when Jack Turner, a handsome guest, comes to her rescue after a man harasses her on the job.

Jack seems like the perfect guy—a successful young lawyer at one of the biggest law firms in the city with charm to spare. The only problem is, Victoria's deep-seated hatred for lawyers. Despite her growing feelings for Jack, she can't bear to get too close to him in case he turns out to be just as rotten as the lawyers from her past. As Jack falls more and more for Victoria, he realizes that his relationship is more complicated than he could have ever imagined, and he faces a difficult choice—to choose between the well-being of one of his clients or his growing feelings for Victoria.

Will they unravel the tangled web of their past and present and heal after a lifetime of pain? Or allow their past to keep them apart?

For Lea,
shine bright little one.

PROLOGUE

"HEY, LITTLE MAN," I said, walking into a cold, bleached room with a large window that looked out to the neighboring rooftop.

Though I had been in and out of health facilities my whole life, I'd never seen a room with an impressive entertainment system that comprised of a flat screen TV tucked away in a dark blue–painted cabinet. Didn't surprise me though. Luke's mother was a lawyer and spared no expense in redecorating Luke's private room. Then again, if I had a sick child, I would do anything I could to make their stay feel less of an institution and more like home.

"Vicky, I missed you!" Luke said, sitting up in his hospital bed, playing a video game.

I was his favorite junior volunteer—or that was what I told myself. He always knew how to make me laugh or brighten my day. Ironic since I was the one supposed to visit patients like Luke in case they needed someone to talk to, so they didn't feel so isolated. It was a five-hour shift a week, but I sometimes did more than that, depending on my work schedule. I enjoyed being here because it fulfilled me every time I left this building.

I walked closer to Luke's bed, keeping both hands behind my back. "Take your pick," I said.

Luke stroked his chin. "Left!" he said, kicking up his feet.

I revealed the chocolate pudding from my left hand and then placed it on the tray in front of him. "You always guess it. I can't fool you."

I bopped him on the nose, and he giggled. As I watched him chow down, I slowly revealed the second pudding cup from my other hand.

"Surprise." I grinned.

His eyes lit up. "I knew you had another one."

"You have the nose of a bloodhound," I said, sitting in the chair at his bedside. I smoothed out my name tag and tightened the ponytail holding my wavy light-brown hair.

"Vicky?"

I looked up. "What is it, little dude?"

"When do I get to go home?" he asked, putting the empty container on the tray before picking up the second one.

My heart tightened. How was I supposed to respond to him— or any child who asked me that question?

I sighed and then leaned forward to wipe the pudding off his cheek. "I don't have an answer for you, little dude. I wish I did," I said, settling at the edge of his bed. "I know Dr. Stern is working hard to find a treatment that will help you get better. You'll see; you'll be home in no time," I said, wanting more than anything for him to be free from leukemia and back at home with his loving family. It was heartbreaking to witness sick kids like Luke in here. I'd seen a lot because I'd been volunteering at the hospital since the age of sixteen, not long after my brother, Chris, had died.

"That's what Jay said yesterday," the five-year-old boy frowned.

"Jay?" I asked, tilting my head to the side. "Who's Jay?"

"He's my godfather, remember?" He laughed. "I don't talk

about him all the time, but he takes me out to watch baseball games and lets me eat all the junk food I want. He's the greatest," Luke said, eyes studying me for a moment. "You two should meet. Mommy says Jay is single, so he should meet someone nice to hang out with. You're nice ... and you don't have a boyfriend."

"How do you know I don't have someone in my life?" I smiled.

"Because you spend your Friday nights here, at the hospital."

He'd gotten me there. Between my odd jobs and volunteer work, I had no time for meeting new people. Sometimes, I thought I enjoyed being single—maybe too much.

"Oh, Luke," I said, ruffling his hair. "You're sweet to set us up. I hope I get to meet him one day if he's as awesome as you say he is." I was trying to be nice, but the last thing I wanted was to be set up on a blind date by a five-year-old. I was sure Jay was a nice guy, but I had a lot going on right now. Men only complicated things.

"Oh, he is," Luke said. "Can I have more pudding now?"

"A third one? Not today, buddy. Why don't I read you a book until your mom comes by?"

"I don't want a story today," he said with a yawn. "My tummy hurts."

"That's because of all the pudding, silly." I stood and fluffed his pillow. "Try to get some rest, okay? Your parents will be here soon." Quickly, I kissed his forehead and tucked the blankets tighter around him.

As I walked out of the room, I passed the lead doctor in Luke's case. "Hello, Dr. Stern," I said politely.

"Hi," he grumbled, writing on his clipboard. He looked up at me and then toward Luke's room. "Things aren't looking good for him, Victoria. Today, I have to discuss more aggressive treatment options with Luke's parents."

My heart faltered. "I hate to hear that," I said.

"This is one of the worst parts about working at a children's hospital. After all you've been through, why do you continue to volunteer?"

"I love being here," I said, looking over my shoulder at Luke through the open door. "To be able to read stories and make Lego castles with the kids. I just want to see them smile; there's no better reason than that."

"He reminds you of your brother." He looks at me from his steel-framed glasses, and I nod.

Dr. Stern had known my family since my brother, Chris, was first diagnosed with cancer so many years ago.

"Brace yourself, Victoria." He looked at me with pain in his eyes and then continued walking to Luke's room to check on him.

Knots formed in my stomach as I watched Luke's bubbly personality shine through as the doctor asked him about his video game. I had a hard time moving on to the next room. Luke had a special spot in my heart, and it saddened me that he had to go through all this. He was such a good kid, and he deserved to live out a long and healthy life.

I lingered for a moment. Catching his gaze, I blew him one last kiss before moving to the next room.

1

VICTORIA

ONE YEAR LATER

"Hey, lady!" a man dressed in a gray suit at the end of the bar shouted. "When am I going to get another drink?" he said, each word slurred.

I had the urge to roll my eyes. "You're not next, sir," I said as I poured wine for two older women.

I took my time, chatting with one of the ladies about her beautiful pink diamond ring she'd gotten as part of her divorce settlement. And though the ring was an impressive piece of jewelry—a nineteen-carat, rectangle-cut gemstone—there was not one inch of me that was envious.

The ballroom where the event was taking place was in the Masterson Hotel, the most popular chain of luxury hostelry in the world. Round tables spread out across the room, filled with wealthy people chatting about world events or what items they would be bidding on in tonight's auction.

I dreaded working at this event, but my roommate and best friend, Scarlett, had pushed me out of bed that morning. The two of us worked together at Florence Catering, which was okay, but I hoped to earn enough money, so I could one day start my full-service catering and event firm.

For tonight, I poured drinks at a fundraiser for the New York Children's Hospital. After Luke's death, I couldn't bring myself to volunteer there anymore. Losing Luke had been like losing Chris all over again. I had lost a friend, someone I'd really cared about.

I kept my back to the angry man until he shuffled down the bar and sat next to the old women.

"Excuse me!" he slurred, swaying slightly. "You get paid to serve drinks, not socialize with these old hags."

One lady with a large black purse swatted his shoulder before stomping off with her drink, and the other splashed her champagne in his face, which he seemed unaffected by. I placed a napkin in front of him and bit the inside of my cheek to stop myself from laughing before turning away. The delicate piano music echoed through the ballroom, barely diminishing the sounds of his shouts. I looked up at the chandelier above my head, listening to the man pound his fist against the counter, and wondered how much longer this was going to last. *Was he ever going to go away?*

"Sir, with the way you're behaving, you don't deserve to be served anymore. You couldn't even wait for me to finish with those two lovely women, and if you can't treat me with respect, I will have to call security,"

"You're the help," he said, and I finally made eye contact. "You should know how to do your job or else I know people who can get you fired in a heartbeat. Give me another scotch."

He waved his glass in front of my face, and I snatched it from him.

"You're cut off."

"Give that back!" He flung himself across the bar, reaching

out for me, when someone wrenched him back, yanking him by the collar.

My eyes locked with the man who had come to my aid.

Who was this? My knight in shining armor? Honestly, I didn't need one.

I studied his smooth skin, dark eyes, and slick black hair. He wore a tuxedo—expensive, fitting him in all the right places. He had a five o'clock shadow that outlined his perfectly chiseled jawline.

I had just possibly laid eyes on the handsomest man in the room, but that was something I would keep to myself.

"Go back to your wife, Anthony," he said, shoving the intoxicated man away. He sat on a barstool and fixed the cuffs of his blazer. "Sorry about that," he sighed. "He's not a bad guy, but his drinking gets out of hand at these things. Someone should have warned you."

"Don't worry about me. I can hold my own," I said, cleaning out a glass. "What can I get you?"

He shook his head. "Nothing for me. I promised my date I would drive her home, which was a huge mistake. She's boring, and she has the urge to fill the silence with some kind of noise or random fact. When I saw you being harassed by that animal, it gave me the perfect excuse to slip out of her sight."

"How nice of you." I blinked.

I took it back; he wasn't even the best-looking man in the world.

"Can I hide out here with you?" He flashed me a smile.

Was he flirting with me? I had been working all these odd jobs and kept myself too busy to ever notice if anybody was paying attention to me.

"You can do whatever you want; it's a free world. But I can't promise you I'll be more entertaining."

I winked, opening a beer bottle for a short man who had been coming to me all night. I slid it across the counter to him, and he slapped another twenty-dollar bill down, which I tucked into the pocket of my black polyester pants. When the short man disappeared, I glanced back at my new friend, who was still staring at me. I felt the heat rise up the back of my neck. This guy made me feel like I was a feast for one's eyes, and I didn't mind it.

Not at all.

"So, why did you invite her to an event like this if she's so boring?" I let out a low laugh, wiping down the counter.

"I hate coming to these fundraisers alone, especially when I'm always given a plus-one. I usually pick up an intern from the office or hit up a bar beforehand," he said.

I paused and glanced at him, wishing he'd stop talking. He was ruining it for me. I always told Scarlett, the more attractive a man was, the less interesting he became, and this guy sitting in front of me was no better.

"Sounds lonely." I raised my brows.

A little pathetic, but I didn't say that out loud.

"I really don't care." He shrugged. "As long as it makes for a great photo. I'm hoping to win that boat—or at least buy it from the person who does."

"It's an auction," I said firmly. "Do you even know what this fundraiser is for?"

He looked up at me with fire in his eyes. "Don't assume I'm some half-wit who only comes here for overpriced alcohol and pointless conversation. I do care about these events, and my reputation is important to me."

Oh, I get it. He's one of those. A trust-fund baby with too much time and money that he didn't even know what to do with himself. He showed up to these kinds of events, so he had a purpose in his life—pretending he was making a difference in the world, but all he cared about was being seen in an overpriced suit.

"So, what do you do for a living?" I asked, crossing my arms.

"Have you been spending the last ten years of your life blowing your trust fund?" I said as Mr. Tall, Dark, and Handsome flashed me a smile, like I'd amused him or something.

I should watch how I talked to the guests, but when I met these uptight jerks, they brought out the worst in me. Maybe because they reminded me of my father.

"I'm just like you," he said, pulling a business card out of his wallet and tossing it at me. "I earned my place at Brookman Farlow Turner Lit Law Firm, and I didn't use anyone's help to get it."

The gorgeous meter just dropped to a negative gazillion. Too bad. This had started out well.

So much for the sunset on the horizon.

"You're a name partner, huh?" I said looking at the card before I chucked it into the trash can at my feet. "Don't you high-powered attorneys always have fancy cars and chauffeurs to drive you around town? It frees up some of your time, so you can continue keeping corporate criminals out of jail." I smirked.

"So, you've heard of us?" he asked with a grin. "I'm the Turner of the firm—Jack Turner."

He held out his hand, but I ignored it.

"Everyone in New York has heard of you. I think your firm is filled with a bunch of snakes, repeatedly poisoning the world with each corporate criminal you set free."

Too much? Yep, that should get me fired.

"Aren't you sassy?" The look in his eyes made me think he was enjoying this. "So, you don't like lawyers."

Mr. Hotshot had no idea.

"No, not one bit."

"Pity," he said as his eyes trailed over me. He let out a low breath. "I'm just trying to make a living," he scoffed. "You know what? Pour me a whiskey. My date can find her way home."

"I'm not serving you now that I know you're driving."

"I'll call one of my drivers to get me. That's what I get for letting them have the night off, so I could take out my new Ferrari." He was mocking me. "Whiskey. Pour it."

I stared at him with an icy gaze. "No."

Jack stood, rubbing his temples. "I don't need to take this crap. The second half of the auction is beginning soon." He walked away, paused, and then turned back. "Look, I don't need this high-and-mighty attitude from you. I paid my way through law school, and I chose the life I have because I'm good at what I do. I work damn hard for it. You might not agree with the way business ethics are run in New York, but you have no idea how much crap I sift through every day to make my clients happy. So, you can sit here on your barstool throne and think you're better than me, but don't think you know the type of man I am because my name is on the side of a building that you don't like."

We stared at each other for a moment, my eyes wide.

I cleared my throat and ruffled my hair. "You're right, Mr. Turner; it was unfair of me to judge. Would you like that drink now?" I hated him even more, but I had to be nice if I wanted to keep my job.

Jack sat in front of me and extended his hand again. "Let's start over. Hi, I'm Jack."

"Victoria," I said, shaking his hand.

"Victoria what?"

"Is my last name necessary?" I frowned. I knew, the first chance he got, he'd notify my boss about the crappy service. And, by tomorrow morning, I would be looking for a new job—one of many anyway.

"I think it tells a story about a person."

I raised my eyebrows. "Really?"

"No, I'm kidding. It's more of a habit," he replied. "The name makes it easier to dig up dirt on them."

I knew it. The man is a snake.

"I'm an open book, and I can tell you with one hundred percent certainty that I don't have any dirt for you to dig up. Sorry." I shrugged.

"What's your name then?"

"Victoria Fairfax." I shifted my chin up.

"Fairfax? Like the—"

"Yes, my grandfather is a big-time real estate developer. Ironic, huh? My family is richer than you are, but here I am, serving you."

"So, I guess you're the one who's a trust fund baby," he said, fiddling with the gold watch around his wrist.

"Hardly," I scoffed. "I'm cut off from my father's side of the family."

"Why is that?"

"Get one of your interns to research me if you're so curious," I said.

"I thought you were an open book?"

"Limited-time offer." I grinned.

"I should get back," he said. "If you ever need my help, fish my card out of the trash."

"I know your name. I'll figure it out." Flipping the towel over my shoulder, I watched him walk away.

Until midnight, I served drinks for the wealthiest socialites in New York City, envying their ability to give back so much to the hospital. I didn't care about their clothes, diamonds, or expensive items they bid on. All I wanted was to pour them drinks, so they'd be too drunk to know they were offering outrageous amounts.

AT THE END of the night, I stood on the sidewalk in my long black trench coat, waiting for Scarlett to bring the car around. Suddenly, I heard high-pitched laughter behind me. I found Jack guiding his date into a black town car. Who knew that a gentleman was hiding inside a big ogre? As I rubbed my arms at the cold breeze surrounding me, I felt a tap on my shoulder.

Turning, I saw Jack.

"I hope you get your date home safe," I said.

"She gets less interesting with alcohol," he teased. "I'd better get her home before she talks about algebra—or hurls in my car," he murmured.

"Have a good night," I said, sensing a strong awkwardness between us.

I swung back, but he stopped me by placing a hand on my shoulder.

"Your father's side of the family doesn't know what they're missing," he said and walked away.

I peered at his back, confused. He didn't know me, so why would he say something like that? I moved up to the edge of the sidewalk when Scarlett pulled up in her blue sedan. I got in, settled into my seat beside her, and then shut the door.

"Seat belt," Scarlett said like a scowling mom.

"Right."

I fumbled to put it on as Scarlett sped off, taking us to our tiny apartment in Brooklyn.

WHEN I UNLOCKED THE DOOR, the spoiled scent of left-over pizza stung my nose. "Scar, I thought you would clean this up before our shift," I whined.

Scarlett moved the trash off the couch and laid it down on the floor. "You could have done it since it bothers you."

"I shouldn't have to," I said, dropping my purse by the door. "It's not my mess."

If only I could afford a place of my own, then I wouldn't have to subject myself to Scarlett's lifestyle. I mean, I loved the girl, but sometimes, I felt like I was being taken advantage of. She had no respect that I lived here, too. That was why I'd stopped cleaning up her mess a long time ago.

"I'll tidy up tomorrow," she huffed, clicking the remote to turn on the television.

The loud voice of the newscaster filled our apartment, making me cover my ears. Quickly, she turned it down, but the woman who lived beside us was already banging on the wall.

"You'd better. This place is looking like an episode of *Hoarders*," I said, pouring myself a glass of wine. I moved her feet and then sank into the cushion. "We need to go out," I said, reminding myself that, on Friday, it would have been a year since Luke had passed away.

"No, actually, you need a man, honey. Your work is consuming your life."

"That's sexist of you." I scowled. "I'm too independent. If I had space in my life or the desire to date, I would. Right now, I want to focus on saving up to start my business. I hate that you think I *need* someone to be happy." I directed my eyes at her. "You're single, and you're happy."

"I'm also in a no-strings-attached relationship," she said, flipping her blonde hair over the armrest. She smiled and innocently batted her long lashes at me. "I have fun with my life. Where's your fun?"

It was probably trapped under that pizza box sitting on the floor.

"I'm working to achieve my goal. That's fun." I smiled.

"Working all these odd jobs will not get you any closer to your dreams, and volunteering is work with no pay—it's useless."

"The reward is—"

"Spare me." She then threw a pillow at me and sat up straight. "Last year, it broke you," she said, poking my arm with her toes. "I don't want to see you go through that again," she added. "Why don't I set you up with someone?"

"A blind date? No, thanks," I said, swirling my wine.

"Yes, with my cousin Patrick. He's smart and handsome."

"He lives here in New York?"

"Patrick just moved down about two years ago from Rochester."

"I've never heard you talk about him before." I raised my brow.

"Vicky, I have twenty-three cousins. I'm not going to talk about all of them," she huffed.

"I appreciate that you're concerned, but I don't think meeting a stranger in a half-lit bar is something I need right now," I said.

Scarlett shuffled closer, gripping my hand. She looked me in the eye and smiled. "You're my best friend, and I'm so proud of us for making our way to New York and living our dreams."

"But?"

"But, if you don't get off your ass and do something for yourself, I will call your mom and invite her out here."

I gasped. "You wouldn't dare. Do you know how critical my mother is about everything in my life?"

I had a strained relationship with my mother. All my life, she'd made me feel like she resented me, especially after my brother died. When I'd decided to move out to New York City, I'd thought putting five hours or so between us would do me some good.

"Exactly."

I glared at her and sighed. "Fine, do your worst."

"You won't regret this!" she squealed with excitement and then jumped off the couch.

"Where are you going?" I groaned.

"I need to call him right now!"

"It's two in the morning," I said, looking at my watch. "No one wants a call this early."

"Right," she sighed, shrugging. "Good night."

"Good night," I replied, stretching out on the couch.

I viewed the television, unable to take in any of the information on the news. *Was I ready to go on a date?* I hadn't been with anyone for eighteen months, ever since I'd broken up with Brook. I guessed I was about to find out.

2

VICTORIA

ON FRIDAY, I sat at a corner table across from Scarlett's cousin Patrick. I'd decided five minutes ago that I would tune him out. All I had to do was sporadically murmur a few words like *uh-huh* or *right* as I chewed my food, and he would keep on chatting about how he loved to work out. He had a nice body, so I was baffled by his need to point out how other women found him attractive. For example, he used to work for a security company, and he told me how women would ogle him in his uniform.

What would I do with that piece of information?

Narcissistic jerk. Abort, abort!

Well, at least I felt no pressure to impress him, and I definitely didn't need to worry about being rude for not listening as he kept going ...

Oh my God, did he call himself Adonis?

Why did I listen to Scarlett?

I'd never gone on a blind date before, and now, I knew why. At least it gave me a chance to soak in the atmosphere of the four-star restaurant that was impossible to get reservations without Scarlett. Last month, she'd filled in for a sick hostess over a weekend, gaining favor with the owner, who knew our boss at the catering company. Being the flirty girl she was, I couldn't imagine it was difficult to convince the owner to give us a reservation.

There was a gas fireplace in the middle of the room, surrounded by cushioned chairs for a social circle. Along the walls were red-and-black tables and pictures of obscure landscapes and shapes on the wall. Scarlett had said this was a super-expensive, chic place, but I thought it was over the top for a first date—and luckily, my last one with Patrick.

As I sat there, yawning, I watched a large crowd of businessmen sitting at a long table, drinking and laughing.

To my surprise, I spotted Jack at the end of the table, scrolling through his phone. It was strange that these men would come together to a restaurant as romantic as this one, but it was one of the most sought-after places in the city. I realized I had been staring at him too long when he looked up from his phone and grinned at me. He excused himself from his table and sauntered over.

Oh no. This is going to get awkward.

"Hello," Jack said.

His deep voice caught Patrick off guard.

Looking over his shoulder, he barely got a glimpse at Jack. "Oh, yes! Could we get another bottle of wine sent over? Something relatively cheap but still tasty."

"Um ... Patrick," I said softly, "he's not a waiter. He's my ... acquaintance."

"Only an acquaintance, huh?" Jack asked, placing his hands in his pockets. "You were my feisty bartender. I think that's a step up from acquaintance."

I laughed and looked at Patrick, who stared between us, confused.

"Patrick, this is Jack Turner," I said. "He attended a fundraiser I worked at a couple of nights ago."

"You worked at a fundraiser? I thought your job was at an animal shelter?" he asked.

I frowned. I guessed I wasn't the only one who hadn't been listening.

"Well, I do, but I also work for a catering company, and for this specific event, I was bartending," I said as Jack searched my face.

What was he looking for? Proof I was bored out of my mind? Because I was.

"Jack saved me from dealing with an awful guest," I added sharply.

"That's nice," Patrick scoffed. "I thought you owned your own catering business?"

"No, I told you ... I want to run my catering firm someday." I frowned, and Jack cast me a look.

Jack knew it, and I knew it. This was the worst date ever.

"Anyway, that doesn't sound like fun. You must have been thrilled, working with all those rich stiffs," Patrick said.

This is getting awkward and fast.

"Well, it was good to see you again, Fairfax. Enjoy your evening."

As Jack turned away, Patrick looked at me and said, "Your last name is Fairfax. Is your grandpa ..."

I felt a migraine coming on—a nasty one.

"Yes, he is," I sighed, watching Jack look just as blasé as I did when he returned to his table. "You know, I think it's time for me to go. Would you like me to pay for my half of the bill?"

"Sure, that sounds great!" Patrick added quickly. "Can I walk you home?" he asked as I plopped cash on the table, paying for a meal I'd hardly touched.

"No," I said, pulling on my jacket and wrapping my purse over my shoulder.

I was so turned off right now. I couldn't believe I'd shaved my legs for this.

I said good-bye to Patrick before rushing out of the restaurant. This was the last time I allowed Scarlett to set me up on a blind date—or any date.

Why couldn't I meet someone normal and let things happen organically?

As I walked down the sidewalk, ready to head to Central Park, I heard footsteps rushing up behind me.

"Victoria, hold on."

Looking over my shoulder, I saw Jack. I felt a flutter in my stomach as he grinned.

I mentally slapped myself. *Focus, Victoria. Don't be fooled by that phony smile.*

"Where are you going in such a hurry?"

"Bad date," I said, walking again. "At least I got good food out of it." I was such a liar.

"Can I join you?" he asked, walking briskly to keep up with me. "Are you okay? You're walking funny," he commented.

If I wasn't wearing heels, I would have been far ahead of him. That was what I got for wearing shoes I hadn't touched in two years.

"I can carry you over my shoulders if your feet hurt." One side of Jack's lips went up.

I laughed. "Is that how you get women to come home with you?"

"I would prefer to wine and dine them first. I don't know; maybe that would work, too. Care to try?" Jack smirked.

"Don't you have some corporate big shots to get back to?" I asked with a smile. "I'm sure they're dying to hear about all the cases you've won today. People must swoon over your skills in the courtroom."

"I won nothing because I wasn't in court today, though I am

in the middle of a high-profile case that requires ... and you were teasing me. Right, you don't actually want to hear about this." He zipped up his long coat and stood closer as we walked.

"Why are you here, Jack? If you're looking for a nightly companion, I hope you don't expect it to be me," I said, taking a sharp left. "I'm not that kind of girl."

"I didn't think you were," he said, following me. "You were a good excuse to get away from that boring dinner though."

"Oh?"

"Yeah, I told them you were a cousin and needed someone to walk you home."

"What a bald-faced lie." I chuckled. "I guess that's one of the greatest skills you've learned as an attorney."

"Are you going to keep teasing me about what I do for a living? Because you might not be prepared for the zingers I dish out to you."

"Bring it on," I said, halting. I turned to face Jack in the middle of the sidewalk, interrupting a woman walking her dog.

"What? Here?" he asked, pulling his hands out of his coat pockets to shrug. "I'm more comfortable doing it in the courtroom."

"Pretend I'm the judge," I said, leaning against the bus stop pole. "Give me your worst."

"You're too cute to be a judge," he said, allowing his eyes to glance over me.

"Don't try to get out of it." I grinned. "Show me some of that attorney magnetism. What would you say to me as a judge?"

"I wouldn't insult a judge."

"You must want to though." I raised my brow.

"They're glorified babysitters," he scoffed.

"Aha! I knew you had something awful to say."

"Yeah, but it wasn't directed at you."

"What would you direct at me?" I asked, walking closer to him.

Looking down at me, he remained silent, smiling. "I can't think of anything right now; you're putting me on the spot." He flashed me a charming smile, his eyes slowly taking me in again.

Men.

"If you have a problem with being put on the spot, I can't imagine you're any good of a lawyer," I mused.

"Okay, now, you're just being malicious. I'm a charming guy outside of work. I can't just turn that off when a beautiful girl wants me to insult her. Can I walk you home?"

"That will be a long walk." I divert my eyes up the street before meeting his again.

"Where do you live?"

"Brooklyn. I'm just walking to the train. You can turn back around. I'm sure your buddies miss you." I continued to walk and then turned another corner, reaching the staircase to the subway. "This is where I leave you." I cast him a side-glance.

"No way."

"Excuse me?" I raised my eyebrows and grabbed the railing to the stairs. "Are you planning on following me to the train? What about your precious Ferrari?"

"I'm driving a Cadillac tonight." He shoots me that *grin* again.

I hated pretty boys. Especially the ones who knew they were.

"All the more reason for you to leave," I said.

He took my wrist just before I went down the first step. "Let me drive you home. I can't let a beautiful woman in a gorgeous dress go walking on the streets alone."

"I'm not afraid. I can protect myself, thanks," I said, slipping from his grasp and taking a few steps.

He stepped forward, now on the level above mine. I craned my neck to look up at him.

"I think you're getting too defensive," he said, joining me on the step. "I want you to get home safely."

"That's very nice of you, but we don't know each other."

"We could." He smiled wolfishly.

"I think we should forget about our little bonding experience at the fundraiser and move on."

"Is there anything wrong in me wanting to get to know you? We can be friends if that's all you're after."

He stumbled closer, pressing his body against mine. I could smell strong hints of alcohol on his breath that made me think he'd had one too many.

"There's no way in hell we would ever be friends. We don't run in the same circles. You attend fancy events while I work to cater them. Our similarities begin and end there."

"Okay"—he laughed—"you're getting angry for no reason. Why don't we go back up to the street and get drinks to relax you?"

"Drinks? Are you serious? How many have you had?" I frowned.

"One … three maybe? I don't even feel a buzz yet." He shrugged. "Come back to my place; you'll love my apartment on the Upper West Side. It has two bedrooms and a panoramic view of the city."

"No, I—"

"You must be looking for someone more exciting than that guy back there. Let me show you a good time."

Good time? No, thanks.

This guy had no clue that my idea of a good time was to slip into my white terrycloth robe and dig into the leftover dessert that Scarlett had brought home from last night's party. A rich chocolate cake filled with toffee, caramel, and whipped cream. It was actually called Better Than Sex.

"Something tells me you won't remember this tomorrow," I

sighed, pushing him off and continuing my descent to the bottom of the staircase.

At the last step, I paused and looked back at him. He stood still, his hands in his pockets. A maternal instinct kicked in, and I couldn't leave him wandering the streets alone in this condition.

As I walked back up, he winked at me.

"I see you came to take me up on my offer."

"No," I said, linking my arm with his. "I'm putting you in a cab. You can find your car tomorrow when you're sober."

"I'm fine."

"Evidently, you're not," I said, feeling his weight pushing me down. I tried to straighten him out, but he kept leaning into me.

"Maybe you're right ... it's suddenly hitting me." He rubbed his face.

I exhaled. "Come on, hotshot. Let's get you home," I said as we stumbled down the street.

"Jeez, how much do you weigh?" I asked, wrapping my hands around his shoulders, trying to get a good handle on him.

"You're enjoying this, huh? It's been a while since I've been fondled this much."

"Don't get excited, Jack." I tugged on the sleeve of his coat harder, giving him a side-glance. "You don't strike me as a man lacking physical attention."

"Well, it's been ... awhile." He shrugged.

"What? You mean as in ... you haven't ... with a woman ... celibate?" I let out a giggle when he nodded. "Sorry, I didn't mean to laugh—" I put my hand to my mouth. "It's just ... well ... you."

"I know it's difficult to believe, but yes, a whole year—why am I telling you this?" He chuckled to himself. "It's not that I haven't had the opportunity because I've had plenty." He cleared his throat. "It's just that I haven't met someone who can turn the switch back on, so to speak."

"Just to clarify ... you mean getting it up?" I asked.

His silence said everything.

"I'm sorry. It's not any of my business," I said, diverting my eyes back on the street.

"Don't apologize."

I wasn't sure if it was the alcohol talking, but it was surprising that he was telling me something very personal.

A total stranger.

What kind of man would tell a woman he hadn't had sex in ages ... unless he was trying to get me to feel sorry for him. Maybe that bullcrap lie would work with other women but not me.

One thing was for sure; Jack Turner would never get into my pants. That was his main objective, right? He was a lawyer after all. A conniving and manipulative kind. Sure, he was very attractive, but I'd vowed to myself a long time ago that I would never, *ever* date a lawyer. Even if he was the last man on earth and there was a huge shortage of Better Than Sex cake, I would still stay away.

At least, I hoped.

Then, I realized something else about Jack. All these random women he brought to these charity events were probably an act. Jack Turner had a reputation to maintain in New York; he was a playboy. And, if he was telling the truth about his issues of not being able to perform in the sheets—which I doubted—it would be because of a deeper issue or some sort of emotional disorder. Then, I'd guess he was more human than I'd thought he was.

We stopped walking when I caught sight of a yellow cab coming in our direction. I flagged down a taxi and pushed Jack inside.

When he was seated, Jack peered up at me. "You sure you don't want to come?" He raised a brow, and a wolfish grin spread across his face.

"It's okay to be by yourself, Jack. Being alone doesn't make you a loner, and sometimes, you just need to embrace it."

He thought about it for a split second before meeting my eyes again. "Good night, Victoria."

"Take care of yourself, Jack," I said. Then, I called out to the driver, "Take him home." I shut the door and watched it drive away.

What a night.

3

VICTORIA

LATER, when I got home, I changed into my pajamas and collapsed on my bed in my tiny room. In the corner, clothes were folded on my chair because I'd stuffed my closet with unpacked boxes full of books and memorabilia from my childhood. As I stared at the ceiling, hoping I wouldn't get set up on another blind date for as long as I lived, Scarlett burst into my room.

"What are you doing home, Vicky?" she asked, her shrill voice piercing my eardrums. "You're supposed to be out, having the time of your life. You realize it's only ten o'clock?"

I groaned, sitting up to lean against the wall. I flicked on my lamp and saw Scarlett standing in the doorway with her arms crossed.

"Patrick called. He said you ran out on him." She squinted at the light and then climbed into bed beside me.

Served him right!

"Sorry, Scarlett. I know he's your cousin, but we didn't click," I said as she rested her head on my shoulder.

"I was so sure you would like Patrick."

"Really? What did you think I would like about him? The

fact that he thinks every woman on earth wants him? The entire time we spent together, he didn't ask a single thing about me."

She wrapped her arms around me and kissed my cheek. "He talks a lot when he's nervous. He must really like you."

In love with himself is more like it.

"The guy was obnoxious," I said.

"I'm going to set up another date for you guys." She shoved her finger in my face, and I pushed it back to her side. *Jeez how many drinks did she have?*

"Nope, that won't be necessary." I gave her a side-glance. "No offense, but there's only so much I can take of listening to a man talk about dumbbell flyes versus standing cable crossovers flyes," I said, moving her hair away from her face.

"Flyes? What are flyes?" she mumbled.

"Something to do with weight lifting, I think. Anyways," I sighed, "I know you're looking out for me, but I don't think it'll work out with Patrick. Not to mention, this other guy was trying to hit on me after I left the restaurant. I've had my fair share of men for a while."

Why am I mentioning Jack? So unnecessary, Victoria.

"What?" Scarlett squealed. She turned to face me, sitting cross-legged. "There was another guy? Who was he?"

I laughed, shaking my head at her excitement. "His name is Jack Turner. I met him at that fundraiser we worked at a few nights ago. Decent conversationalist, but he's just a player. That's not my type. He's a big jerk when he's drunk, too. Well ... I guess he wasn't the worst, but it wasn't great."

Scarlett's jaw dropped. "Jack Turner hit on you? That steamy attorney we saw on the news?"

I nodded. "He's all right, but Jack is, like, thirty-five. Way too old for me."

"Older men are where it's at, girl!" she exclaimed, shoving my shoulder. "Snatch this guy up before someone else takes him."

I hate this version of Scarlett when she's tipsy. I should put her to bed.

"He's not the settling-down type," I said, getting out of bed. "He's just a playboy who enjoys playing with cars. I don't need that in my life. I want something more meaningful."

"Whatever," she grumbled, and I helped her stand.

"Where did you guys go tonight?" I asked, considering she was home way too early.

I knew that Scarlett had gone out with a few girls we worked with at Florence Catering. I would have gone out with them tonight if I hadn't agreed to go on that blind date. Now, I wished I had.

"We went to Newbie Bar. You should have come along. Maybe you would have had a better time." Scarlett yawned.

"You think?" I draped her arm over my shoulders and walked her to her room.

"So, you're not seeing Patrick again?"

"Nope," I said, making it clear.

"And Jack Turner?"

"Definitely not. I won't be seeing Jack again; trust me. Tonight was a fluke, but if I see him, I'll let him know you're interested."

"Perfect!" she said as I tucked her under her fleece blanket. "You're the best friend of all the best friends I have. I love you, baby." She wrapped her arms around me and tried to kiss my lips.

"All right, Scarlett, I think you need to sleep this off." I slipped out of her grasp and then returned to my room.

I tried to think about the day when I would have my own clean apartment, paying for it with the money I earned from running my catering company. But, for whatever reason, my thoughts kept drifting to the hotshot attorney and wondering whether he'd made it home okay.

4

VICTORIA

FOR THE NEXT FEW WEEKS, I went on working as many hours as I could, saving my money to one day open VF Catering Services—or VS, if I could convince Scarlett to be on board with me. I could take care of the food while she took care of booking events. But Scarlett, though I loved her, couldn't commit to anything.

The sun shone that afternoon, and there were only a few clouds in the sky. I was standing under a tent, working at a long table, serving burgers off the grill, while dressed in my favorite blue tee with a brown dog on it, getting many compliments from the kids. The rescue dogs played in a park nearby while the families gathered to see if they wanted to adopt any. I was in the environment I always wanted to surround myself with—family and love. Although I had a family, I never felt the closeness . . . or felt wanted, for that matter.

As I continued to serve hamburgers, an eerie feeling came over me, like someone had been watching my every movement.

"Good afternoon, sir," I chirped before the realization slapped me in the face. "Would you like vegan or ..." I looked up from the grill, and my huge smile faded. The world got a little darker as I realized who was next in line. I dropped my steel tongs on the table covered in plastic. "We need to stop meeting like this," I said with a hesitant smile.

He fixed the cuffs of his dress shirt and then stuffed his hands in his pockets. He looked way too formal for a family picnic, but I didn't think he knew any other style.

"Well, it's a pleasure to see you, too," he said softly, grabbing a paper plate from the side of the table. "I'd like a real burger, none of that vegan or tofu crap." He held out his paper plate with an open bun and gestured with his eyes for me to plop a hamburger patty. "Cute shirt."

I glanced down at my top, and then my eyes flicked back to Jack. "Thanks. The kids like it, but you don't get to look at Rover. He's for nice people." I smirked.

"Hey, I thought we were on good terms. You put me into that cab, remember?"

"Yes, I did." My lips went thin.

"You could have left me on the street."

"I could have—and wanted to, believe me," I said, handing the tongs to my colleague.

"But you didn't—because you cared." He eyed me, amused.

"That's very presumptuous of you." I snorted.

"I call it the way I see it." He offered me a wicked grin.

I huffed, turning to the girl next to me. "Debbie, I'm taking my ten-minute break," I told her, placing a baseball cap on my head before I stepped out into the sunlight, walking toward the park.

Jack raced after me, grabbing my arm and pulling me to look up at him. "Can you stop walking and allow me to apologize for being such a jerk?" he asked.

Looking into his eyes, I could tell that he meant it.

"Not that I care ... and I'm more curious than anything else, but why the sudden binge?" I asked curiously.

Jack's eyes remained focused on his feet for a short moment before he finally had the courage to lift them up to mine. "I was having a hard time with an anniversary of something terrible, and if I didn't follow you out, I would have probably drunk enough to make me forget about it."

"An anniversary of your divorce?" I scoffed.

I thought he would laugh, but his eyes filled with sadness, and he lowered his head. "No, that would be cause for celebration," he said. "This was much more tragic. I was never married, but I was close. My soon-to-be wife died by choking on a chicken bone. I was in the next room, and she couldn't call out for me. The game was blaring on the television, and there was no way for me to know she was turning black and blue."

I blankly stared at him, my arms folded. "You almost had me there for a second."

"What gave me away?" he asked, sniffling and patting fake tears from his cheeks.

"Your tone of voice and the fact that I saw that same story on the news last night. How can you be okay with using someone's tragedy as your own?" I shoved him—or at least tried to. The man was a beast. "Do you know what loss feels like?"

"I lost the keys to my favorite car yesterday. Does that count?"

"Hardly. You're an asshole," I said, looking him up and down. "You're a little overdressed for a picnic."

"But it caught your attention." He grinned. "I came here straight from work. A friend of mine is a veterinarian, and he always asks me to come out to these things. Ironically, he's not here himself." He glanced around before his eyes met mine.

"Are you talking about Dr. Winters?" I asked, and he nodded.

"There was an emergency back at the clinic. He had to rush out of here a few minutes ago."

"That sounds like him," Jack said.

"Something you can't relate to, I'm sure."

"Why do you hate me so much?" He laughed. "I thought you were giving me a chance."

"You thought wrong." I continued walking, pivoting away from the dog park to throw him off.

He still followed, matching each stride I took. I crouched near a bench where a woman sat, reading, with her golden retriever on a leash.

"What an adorable dog!" I squealed. "Do you mind if I pet him?"

The woman took off her sunglasses and smiled at me. "As long as you don't mind getting attacked by his slimy tongue."

"Nope, not at all," I replied.

I laughed, rubbing his back and behind his ears. The dog leaped, sending me on my back. I giggled uncontrollably as the dog wagged his tail and licked me to death.

"You're such a cutie," I said in a high-pitched voice. Looking over my shoulder, I asked, "Do you want to pet him?"

"No, thanks," he said, shaking his hands in front of his chest. "Dogs are not my thing."

"Yet you came for a picnic at a dog park. You are one big mystery, Jack Turner." I stood, brushing the grass and dog saliva off my hands. I settled into a bench beside the woman and continued watching the dogs and children play in the field. Seeing a little boy who reminded me of my brother when he was a kid churned a maternal instinct inside me.

"Kids," Jack said, sitting next to me.

I groaned. "You made your apology, so you don't have to follow me around like a lost puppy—no pun intended."

"I'd like to take you out. There's a charity event coming up for children in developing countries. You deserve a night where you can wine and dine. It will be my treat. It'll be my thank-you for not abandoning me on the side of the road."

Will this man ever give up? I wish he would.

"That sounds uncharacteristic of you," I huffed. "No, thanks. I don't need to be the next eye candy wrapped around your arm because Jack Turner is afraid to be alone."

"I'm not afraid of being alone." His eyebrows shot up.

"You keep telling yourself that, hotshot."

He chuckled before saying, "You have to let me do something."

"Why?" I asked, turning to him. "We're squared. You owe me nothing. What I did last night was what any sensible human being would have done. I did the right thing, putting you in a cab. I wasn't trying to save your life but someone else's." I winked at Jack, imitating his smooth class. "Catch you later, hotshot."

As I walked away, he called out, "How about friendly drinks?"

I whirled around.

"You don't have to look at me or talk." He smiled, and it was contagious.

"That's absurd." I hiked my brows.

"We can go to a bar of your choice," Jack added, trying to sweeten the deal.

What was this guy about?

I'd bet he wasn't used to this kind of behavior from women. They probably said yes to everything Jack asked from them, and he didn't know how to handle rejection.

"You might regret that," I said, stepping forward. "I'll make you a deal. At the end of this event, there will be a relay race that requires all adults to participate. We'll go on separate teams, and if my team wins, then you have to leave me alone—for good." I playfully raised my shoulder.

"And if I win?"

"I'll take you up on that friendly drink." I extended my hand before Jack shook it.

There was no way he would win in a pantsuit. Then, I had a vision of Jack splitting his pants wide open, and I had to bite my bottom lip, stopping myself from laughing out loud.

"What's so funny?" He glanced at me with curiosity.

"Nothing," I said, clearing my throat.

"You'll regret challenging a man like me."

"Just because you're talented in your career doesn't mean you're good at running."

"Track in high school will help though," he threw at me.

I narrowed my eyes. "You're bluffing."

He shrugged. "You just wait and see," he said over his shoulder, walking away from me.

FOR THE REST of the afternoon, I helped clean up the leftover food and pack the tables back into the van. I was surprised to find Jack helping us out. It wouldn't surprise me if he billed the animal shelter for his time. Nobody worked for free, especially a man like Jack.

Or maybe he was doing this to impress me, but if he were, he had another thing coming.

They brought some of the dogs that weren't adopted back to the shelter. I wished I could bring them all home with me, but my lease didn't permit me to have even one. Next, we all gathered in the open field and then split into teams of three for the relay race. Jack and I, on our respective teams, would be the ones to run to the finish line.

As the director of the event explained the rules, I shook out my limbs and bounced on my toes. I wiped sweat from my brow and fanned myself with my shirt. Looking over at Jack, I saw he was relaxed, barely in a ready-to-run stance. I smirked, staring at him until he looked at me. He shot me a death glare, and I knew he wasn't about to let me win. I doubted he could run that fast in dress pants, but he seemed relatively fit for a thirty-five-year-old lawyer.

The noise blasted in my ears as the director blew the whistle. My first team member instantly took off while the dad on Jack's team took his time. My heart pounded as I waited for the baton to slap against my palm. Ahead of me, at the finish line, two little girls held the rope for us to run through. The five teams were firmly tied, but my second team member was a hair ahead of the pack.

Finally, the baton was mine, and I took off like a shot. I pumped my legs, never looking away from the rope. Out of the corner of my eye, I saw Jack coming toward me. He was slow, sloth-like, and then, just as I reached out to touch the rope, Jack crashed through it and pumped his fists in the air. His teammates congratulated him while I rested my hands on my thighs, panting. My face was red as I caught my breath, watching Jack making his way toward me.

"What the hell was that?" I asked Jack, straitening myself back up and met his eyes. "You came out of nowhere."

"You should hit the gym a little harder next time, short stack," he said, pinching the loose skin on my arm. "Learn to pace yourself, too, or else you'll wear out faster than an old man."

"Like you?" I said.

He chuckled. "I look good for an old man, don't you think?" He played with the top buttons of his shirt.

"Maybe—for a man who cheated," I huffed, though I had no evidence to support that.

"Sore loser?" he asked, nudging my side. "Where am I taking you for drinks?"

"No. No way that's happening," I said, painfully aware of my denial. "I let you win to boost your ego. I have no intention of ..." I lost my train of thought, and my eyes followed his hand as his fingers fumbled on the last button of his oxford shirt.

"We shook on it." Jack flapped his open shirt to cool off, exposing his tan skin.

I fought the urge to reach out and touch the curve of his stomach.

Jeez, how many hours did he spend working out? I should sign up at a gym. Dumbbell flyes or standing cable crossovers flyes? I wished I'd paid attention to Patrick.

"Well, I never said when I would go out with you," I replied, desperately looking for a way out. "I'll look at my calendar and see if I have any free time, but don't hold your breath."

"You're scared of me. Scared that, given a chance, you might like me," he said, standing closer.

"What?" I laughed a little too hard, making it sound fake. "There is nothing about you I'm afraid of, Jack. You're insane."

"Name-calling. A perfect indication you have no viable evidence to refute my claims, so you revert to insults."

"Don't lawyer me," I said, walking to the parking lot to make a getaway in Scarlett's sedan that she'd lent me to come to this event.

Jack followed me, running backward to face me. "You're scared of my intellect and my charm, aren't you? Maybe you've never had a high-profile friend like me before."

"I've never had a friend with abs like that either, but it's not a prerequisite."

What? Why would I say that?

"So, it's the abs that intimidate you? I promise, they're very friendly." He looked down at his chest before meeting my eyes with a smile.

"I'm not intimidated or looking for a friend, thanks." I

unlocked the driver's door and opened it. Leaning against the doorframe, I watched him sit on the hood of the car.

"I could use a few like you in my life."

"Look, Jack, I'm not interested in making an application. Just leave me alone." I got in the car and honked until he jumped off the hood.

He faced me, blocking the sun out of his eyes with his arm. "I'll meet you at the Greenhouse Pub tomorrow night at nine. If you're not there, I'll keep looking for you until I get what I'm owed. Don't forget to wear something sexy!"

He waved as I backed out of my spot and sped away. I so wanted to flip him the bird, but I didn't because I was a lady.

WHEN I GOT HOME, I dropped my bag by the door and was ready to shower.

On the way, Scarlett intercepted me in the hallway. "How was the picnic?"

"Fine."

"Whoa," she said, stepping back, wide-eyed. "I sense you're in a mood. Did something happen?"

"Jack happened," I huffed.

"Jack Turner?"

"The very one," I said, cringing at the thought of his smile— that I wish I could mop the floor with. The man was infuriating. "Jack was such a jerk, trying to apologize for his behavior even though I knew he didn't mean it. Then, he roped me into this stupid bet, and now, I'm supposed to meet him for drinks tomorrow."

"Back up," she said, clutching my shoulders. "Jack Turner invited you out for drinks? Oh, what I wouldn't give to go out with that guy. He's so hot."

"I'm well aware of your feelings for him. You're more than welcome to come along."

Scarlett's mouth dropped open. "You're so wicked! What a good idea. Three is a crowd, right? That would put a damper on the date," she said, repeatedly slapping my arm. "Are you saying I can meet Jack Turner? Don't mess with me, girl. That man is a rock star."

"A rock star?" I chuckled. "Why would you say that? He's just a regular guy. Since when were you so obsessed with him?"

"I've been taking a few law courses online, and my professor says following current events is a great way to broaden your mind."

"Why didn't I know about that?" I asked. So much for our dream of opening a catering firm together.

"It's just a new hobby I picked up in my spare time."

"Tennis is a hobby. Law courses are a career choice." I cast her a look.

"I'm not sure if I'll commit. Let's call it a pastime for now." Scarlett winked.

"You have spare time?" I asked, slipping around her to grab the towel in the closet. "Between work and partying, how is that even possible?" I mused.

"I'm a woman of many talents," she said, flipping her hair back. "So, are we going for drinks with Jack or not? I've been following some of his cases, and he's a genius." She snatched the towel from me and tossed it on the couch.

"I need that."

"Not until you tell me that this isn't a joke."

"I'm trying to get Jack *out* of my life, but I might have to go."

"By going for drinks?"

I sighed heavily. "I lost the bet."

"So?"

"He threatened to find me if I don't show up," I said.

"What if we have a real connection? Then, can I go for it?" Scarlett asked.

I groaned. "How is that going to help me? I told you, I don't want Jack in my life," I said, surprised that I was agitated that she'd asked me that. After a short pause, I gave up. "Fine, as long as you promise not to talk to me about him, you can do whatever you want."

"You're the best." She kissed my cheek and skipped to her room.

I went to the bathroom with knots in my stomach.

5

―――

JACK

HOW LONG HAVE I been staring at the screen?

I couldn't stop thinking about Victoria's eyes, her mouth—what a *mouth*. Every time I was around Victoria, I had the urge to take her into my arms and kiss the hell out of her. The way I saw it, it would serve a dual purpose. First, she would enjoy it. As Victoria would discover, kissing me would leave her breathless, eager for more. And, second, it would make it impossible for her to dish out any of her zingers. I would like to see her try to insult me or my profession after she had a taste of Jack Turner.

My feisty little Victoria.

Something had happened inside me the moment I saw her. I wasn't sure what it was. Love? Not exactly. More like a commotion of feelings that I hadn't sorted out yet. Honestly, I had never felt like that. But I wasn't searching for any kind of commitment because, for me, it was like building a house on a sinkhole. With past experience, I had reached my level of disappointment with love.

Who knew? Maybe Victoria would be the kind of woman to change my mind. I only hoped she was up to the challenge.

I glanced down at my watch—six more hours to go before I got to see that saucy brunette. For the first time in ages, I felt optimistic and excited. It had been a long time since someone caught my attention, and Victoria had all of it.

"Jack, there is a George Fairfax here to see you." My secretary, Helen, came walking into my office. She was fiftyish, with big hair, and wore a Chanel suit—making you believe Joan Collins might have been her idol, growing up. She was a no-nonsense kind of woman and the only one in the office that kept me on my toes. Actually, she was the only one who called me a ruthless bastard on occasions when she didn't agree with my ethics with some clients. That was why I treated people differently. In this business, you couldn't allow personal emotions to get in the way. Otherwise, I would never get paid, and neither would she—even if she didn't need the money. She was married to one of my partners, but Helen was reliable. We worked well together, and that was something you rarely found in this business.

"He's not scheduled to meet me today." I frowned.

"I know, darling, but when a big gun comes storming in, demanding to see you because it's urgent, you have to see what he wants."

"Everything is urgent with Fairfax," I murmured.

The man was a thorn in my backside. There was not a day he didn't call me for something.

"You could spare five minutes; it's not like you're doing anything important right now." She arched her brow.

My eyes went back to my laptop. "I was—"

"Daydreaming," she added and then smiled like she knew something.

"I wasn't, um ... just show him in, please," I huffed, logging off my computer and shoving the file I was supposed to be working on in my drawer.

Helen was wrong, I hadn't been daydreaming. I'd been think-ing. How did I approach this—whatever this was—with Victoria? No point in pretending I was a man who practiced self-restraint. I got what I wanted as soon as I decided I wanted it.

And I wanted Victoria.

"Mr. Turner," George Fairfax said as I stood up from behind my desk.

"Please call me Jack," I said. He might as well since I spoke to him on the phone more than my mother. "What can I do for you today?" I motioned to the chair in front of me before I sat back down.

"Well, as we spoke about my situation on the phone, I want to know if there's anything more you can do for me. My ex-wife is suing me for my inheritance. How can that be possible? We've been divorced for twenty-five years," George said, shifting in his chair.

"You might argue that in court, that the assets were gained long after you had divorced. But, Mr. Fairfax, as I told you over the phone, I'm a corporate lawyer."

"But you're the best," he argued.

He was right; I was. But I had to be confident with every case I took on because I refused to lose.

"I'm well aware that your father's company has been a long-time client at my firm, but I went over the files, and I'm not the suitable person to handle your situation. I can refer you to someone who's more qualified to help you in this kind of—"

"Mr. Turner, maybe I didn't make myself clear. I want no one else." He flashed me an unpleasant look. "And if you're not able to help me, maybe Fairfax Developers Group should find another firm."

George's father's company was one of our biggest clients, and my partners would be unhappy if we lost them as a client. So, this put me in a bind.

"No, that won't be necessary. I suggested it not because I want to keep my hands clean, but because here, at Brookman Farlow Turner Lit Law Firm, we always look out for our clients' best interests." I smiled, pulling out his file from my bottom drawer, where it had been cataloged under Pain in My Derrière.

My eyes skimmed through the pages before glancing back at the rigid man. "All right, if you want me to help you, I need to know everything. No secrets."

"Anything, if it means getting my ex-wife off my back and reconnecting with my daughter," he said.

I leaned back in my chair, watching. "How long has it been since you last saw your daughter?"

He sighed heavily. "My ex, Shannon, was a very manipulative and toxic woman, and she was six months pregnant with my daughter, Victoria, when I filed for a divorce, so—"

"Victoria?" I realized with a jolt that George was Victoria's father.

I had known Victoria had to be the daughter of one of the three Fairfax brothers, but now casting my gaze over at George, how could I not have suspected sooner? Just based on the uncanny resemblance—the high cheekbones, the fair skin and the oval shaped eyes, without a doubt Victoria was his daughter. Only Victoria, being a woman, was far more attractive ... for me anyhow.

"Yes, she's my daughter. I haven't seen her since she was born." His eyelids dropped. "Her whole life, she's been alienated. She knows nothing about me, and her mother did a damn good job of making sure of that."

"But, now that your daughter is an adult, why not try to reach out to her?" I said, meeting his eyes dead on.

"Of course I want to. I always have. Only I'm afraid to go near her, even after all these years. See, my ex-wife had filed a false protection order at the time of our divorce, and if I had contested it, she would have made sure the media would learn of my ventures. I can't imagine what kind of crazy stories she's filled my daughter's head with," George said.

I was not a family lawyer, but I knew enough of what went on in family court. Some women manipulated the system by playing the victim when, in some cases, they were the abuser, as I suspected was the case with George Fairfax.

I sat up in my chair. "What kind of ventures are we talking about?"

"She has proof ... of things." George loosened his blue silk tie.

"Like what?" I drew my brows together.

My time ran a thousand dollars an hour, and on any other day, I wouldn't mind if this lasted forever, but tonight, I wanted to go home early and get ready for my date with Victoria. Now that I thought about it, there was possibly a conflict of interest but only if I took on the case.

George cleared his throat before saying, "I've done things in the past I'm not proud of."

"Mr. Fairfax, I need to know—"

"Drugs, prostitutes," he spat. "In other words, I can't go near my daughter or else Shannon will leak the pictures to the press."

Something twisted in my stomach as I thought of Victoria, who had an extortionist for a mother and a coward for a father. It was a miracle she'd turned out half-decent.

His gaze met mine. "Is there a way of getting around this?" he asked, eyes pleading.

At the time, I had considered sending him to one of my attorney buddies that specialized in family law. But, now, assessing everything, I had other ways to go around this.

I'd learned early on that, if you wanted something, then you made it happen. Might be unethical? Sure. A conflict of interest? For certain. Disbarred? Hopefully not.

I wondered what he would say if he knew I was already

acquainted with his estranged daughter. That my plan B was to construct a relationship with Victoria, but now, my intentions could only be purely business. I would get to know her, and maybe she'd let me in enough for me to get her to convince her thieving mother to drop the lawsuit. Then, everyone would be happy—George, Fairfax Group, the firm, and *me*.

It was not like I hadn't colored outside of the lines before. I was a closer. I got the job done. That was why I was a senior partner at my firm, and I needed to keep my clients happy even if it meant charming the pants off a woman who completely hated my guts.

Besides, if George Fairfax was being truthful, who was I to stand in the way of a father who wanted to get to know his daughter? I needed more time to think of what my next move should be.

"Yes, there could be another way around all this. Give me some time to see what I can do. I'll be in touch."

6

VICTORIA

SCARLETT and I arrived at the Greenhouse Pub around eight thirty. Dressed in jeans and a loose white top, I entered the bar with Scarlett, who wore a red dress that accentuated her curves. She looked great—hot actually. If I were a man, I would be all over her. So, I wondered why it bothered me to know it would take seconds before Scarlett threw herself at Jack, or vice versa. It was because I couldn't stand the man, and I thought Scarlett could do better, right?

The pub was loud with men shooting pool in the corner and sports events on the various television screens. Whether it was on mute or not didn't matter because the sound of clinking glasses and the hearty waves of laughter would have drowned the audio.

We sat in a booth near the entrance with a view of the door to keep an eye out for Jack.

"This place is pretty sketchy," I said, bringing my purse closer to me.

"You're such a snob," she replied. "They have a jukebox. Isn't that fun? This place is not so bad. It could grow on you," Scarlett said, dragging her eyes around the room.

"Or give me hepatitis." I smiled as Scarlett rolled her eyes and then ordered us shots of tequila.

"Be careful," I said, knowing she'd already had a couple of glasses of wine before coming here.

"I know how to hold my liquor," she said, but somehow, I didn't believe her.

We sat there drinking, silent mostly. Then, at nine o'clock, the man of the hour came walking through the door.

"Jack!" Scarlett shouted, and everyone in the bar, including Jack, looked our way.

I placed my hand on my face, thinking to myself that I had created a monster. Could she have waited to be introduced?

"Jack, over here!" Scarlett squealed, standing up and waving her arms.

"Sit down." I laughed, reaching across the table and pushing her into the seat.

Jack approached us, wearing not his usual attire, but dark jeans and a V-neck top. I was impressed. He'd finally taken the time to look up the definition of casual.

"Hello, ladies." He gave me an expression like, *What is going on?* "Don't you look gorgeous this evening?"

He flashed me a fake smile, like I'd caught him off his game. He hadn't expected I would bring a friend who would be there to stop me from doing something foolish tonight—like going home with Jack Turner.

"Jack, this is my friend Scarlett." I beamed.

"Nice to meet you, Scarlett." He leaned over to whisper into my ear, his breath causing shivers to run down my spine, "I was counting on having you all to myself."

The heat rose in my veins. "The more, the merrier, right?" I affirmed.

"For ninety-nine percent of men, this would fulfill some

fantasy, but I have had a long day and was looking forward to it just being the two of us. What a disappointment," he huffed.

When Jack pulled himself away from my ear, his gaze went back to Scarlett.

"So, Scarlett"—he smiled—"what are we having?"

"Water for the rest of the night," I added, casting a look at Scarlett.

She giggled and flicked her wrist. "Jack, come sit beside me." She bounced down the seat to make room and patted the distressed leather.

Smiling, he sat next to her, his eyes never leaving mine as Scarlett clung to his arm like glue.

"You couldn't have picked a better place?" I threw shade at him while nursing my glass of red wine.

"Vicky," Scarlett said, "you're so rude. I'm sure Jack had a long day. Let him sit down and relax."

"It's fine," Jack said, acting as if Scarlett wasn't pawing at him like a juicy steak. "I know she doesn't like me and is taking it out on a great establishment."

"What's so great about it?"

"I used to come here with my college pals," he replied. Then, he ordered us another round of drinks and himself some sparkling water with lime. "We talked about buying it together for the longest time. Then, most of our group moved out of town and got busy with their lives."

"Hey, Jack!" Scarlett shouted louder than necessary. "Did you know I've been taking law courses? I've memorized all the Latin words. *Habeas corpus*. That's pretty good, right?"

Jack looked at me, confused, and I shrugged to prompt him to humor her.

"That's fantastic." He chuckled.

He shot me a look to ask how he did, and I gave him a thumbs-up.

"So, have you given it any thought?" he asked.

"To what?" I leaned forward, switching Scarlett's martini glass with the water.

"Being my date next Saturday. I've got this charity event I told you about—for children in developing countries."

"Oh, right. My answer is still a hard no." I leaned back in my chair, trying hard not to meet his gaze.

"You need a date?" Scarlett chirped. "I'm free."

"Well, I was trying to convince your friend here—"

"You can take Scarlett," I added.

"And you wouldn't mind?" He suspiciously stared at me.

"No. Why would I? We're friends." I held my smile as long as I could while my skin prickled with heat.

"So, it's a date!" Scarlett said.

Jack did nothing, letting her say anything she wanted. She abruptly got up, leaving us alone while she looked at the jukebox in the corner.

"I didn't know we were babysitting tonight," he said, casting his eyes at Scarlett, who was the only one dancing in the room.

"That's not nice, Jack."

"What's not nice is how you brought your friend with you—"

"She wanted to come. What was I supposed to say, no?" I lifted my head to look at him.

"Do you bring Scarlett on all your dates?" His forehead puckered.

"I brought her because this is *not* a date."

"You're right." He looked at me too long, making me feel unsettled. "I was wondering if I could ask you a favor," Jack said. "Not a favor. I'll pay you for it. I'm throwing a poker night for the guys at work and other people I know—nine in total. I was hoping you would cater it."

"Cater a poker night?" I furrowed my brows. "Our company usually only does bigger events. I can jot down a list of names for you though. We've paired with some great local shops that love doing gigs like that." I rifled through my purse for a pen and paper.

"That's unnecessary," he said. "I want you."

I glanced up at him, and something in his words made my heart stop. "I don't freelance."

For a moment, I considered it. If Jack were anyone else, I would jump at the chance, but getting tangled with Jack, even professionally, would be a bad idea.

"It doesn't work that way in catering. I don't think my boss would appreciate it—"

"Here's the deal," he said, leaning forward and resting his hands on the table. "I'm trying to set up a charity, and these men are the biggest investors I know. I need someone like you who can chat them up, pour drinks, and be your charming self." He grinned, and it sounded like I would be paraded like a piece of meat.

I knew it was too good to be true.

"You can hire anyone for that," I said before taking a sip from my glass.

"Tell me what it will take to convince you to do this for me."

I sat back, considering this. "Well, I had planned on starting my catering business someday," I said.

His eyes lit up. "My poker event would be a perfect place to start. There will be rich stiffs, and after they see what you're capable of doing, they will certainly want your services."

"I don't know ..."

"You have a big heart, and I believe you can sell the idea more genuinely to them than anyone. You'd be an asset in making this event successful." He waved a hand in the air. "Just think of how much power you'll have over me. Everything will be your call. The food, the drinks—it will all be up to you." He smiled.

"I like the sound of having power over you." I said through a snort.

"You would." His smile faded. "Just one look, and I knew you would hold my attention, enough to make me do whatever you wanted me to do," Jack said, holding my gaze as my pulse picked up the pace.

"Aren't you getting ahead of yourself? I would need to want you first to do that." I flashed Jack a smug look.

"I love olives!" Scarlett squealed as she made her way back to the table.

I had almost forgotten she was there. She popped an olive in her mouth and licked the inside of the martini glass. The waiter came, asking if we wanted more, and I told him to cut her off. Scarlett groaned.

Suddenly, Scarlet rested her head in her arms and goes quiet.

"Is she sleeping?" I blinked, shocked. "I have never seen Scarlett do that before."

Jack chuckled. "Is she always like this?"

"She's a sweetheart, but the level of fun she craves is outrageous. You probably want her number?" I asked, pulling the lip balm out of my purse. "Since you're taking her out next weekend."

"No, I want yours," he said straight out.

"Not possible," I said without a hesitation, then cleared my throat. "What's the charity?"

"The charity. Right. It's for my friends, in memoriam of their son, someone I was very close to," he said tenderly.

I sensed there was more to the story but didn't push it. "Well, you're in luck. For a long time now, I've volunteered my time at the children's hospital, and I can never seem to bring myself to say no to them or for any good cause for that matter. You're like a little kid, so it must have the same effect."

"Wow, what a dig," he said, clapping slowly. "You've got a sharp tongue. You sure you're not secretly a lawyer?"

"I would rather live in the desert and get eaten by scorpions."

"What if your friend becomes a lawyer?" Jack nudged his head in Scarlett's direction, who was in a deep slumber.

"She won't. She finds a new hobby every few months. This month, it happens to be you."

Jack grinned and came to sit next to me, stretching his arms along the top of the booth. "Your friend is special, but I prefer getting to know her feisty brunette friend instead." His fingers brushed the top of my shoulder. "I'm surprised you didn't invite more people to take advantage of my money."

"She's the only one that matters." I grinned.

"How about I settle the bill and take your friend home, and you come back to my place?"

This was exactly how I didn't want the night to end—tangled up in Jack's Egyptian cotton sheets.

I narrowed my eyes at him. "Can you try not to be a sleaze for one second?"

"Relax. I wanted to talk to you more about the poker night, I swear." He holds up his hands. "Consider it a site visit. We could go over the decor and food," he said. Then, his eyes trailed my face, and he sighed. "I get that you just want to be friends, and nothing with us will ever happen."

I Laughed. "I don't want to be your friend either."

"Business partner then?" he stuck out his hand, and I kept my arms crossed. "I really do need your help with this." He pleaded.

I looked at Jack, and sighed. There was something about him that had me wanting to reconsider, even though I know it's a bad Idea.

"Fine, but more like associates. I don't need a business partner," I said, shaking his hand. "And I have the final say on my paycheck."

"Just throw me a number and consider it done," he said.

"And you must give me a glowing reference if need be."

"I'll praise you to the moon and back." He promised.

"Good," I said, blushing. "Let's drive Scarlett home. We can have the meeting at your place." As I slowly got out of my chair, I realized that now I would be working for Jack. Worst—he would be my boss.

What the hell did I agree to.

Jack paid the bill and then helped me carry Scarlett outside where we met with Jack's chauffeur, an older gentleman wearing a black suit. We piled into the back seat of his town car, Scarlett slumped between us. I stared out the window the whole way to my apartment.

"Do you like this car?" Jack asked.

I glanced up at him, thinking he was trying to engage in a conversation. I didn't believe he cared what I thought about his toy. Or maybe he wanted some validation that I was dazzled by his lifestyle—but I wasn't.

"It's cramped." I stroked Scarlett's hair as she lay, sleeping in my lap.

"There's not usually more than two people in here."

"Really? Hard to believe with the playboy persona you like to project." I scoffed.

"If I wanted to impress the ladies, I'd drive my cars or get my limo. I'm sorry. Are you upset I'm not trying to impress you?"

"I'm exhausted by you," I huffed, nuzzling my head into the cold window. "Stop being your superficial self for two seconds, and then I might actually be impressed."

"What makes you think I'm fake?" he asked in a level tone.

"Because there's something in your eyes." I looked back at Jack's soft, warm eyes, and I felt something familiar in them. "Sadness."

Jack scoffed, "I'm having the time of my life."

"I know that look ... pain and loss." I'd seen it in the mirror many times before—in myself.

"I think you need a little more to drink. You're killing my buzz." Jack smirked.

"What buzz? All you had was sparkling water all night." I arched my brows.

"I'm high on you—"

I rolled my eyes and said, "You're just scared I might see you for what you are."

"And that is?"

My attention whipped back at him.

"That there is more to Jack Turner than meets the eye. You like to hide behind this tough playboy persona. You have this uncontrollable need to maintain an over-the-top reputation because it's a good distraction. It takes the eyes off of, well, you. That way, you don't have to deal with all your baggage."

Jack said nothing, giving me slight satisfaction. That didn't last, quickly transforming into knots in my stomach. I looked at him and the stony gaze that faced straight ahead. I knew there was something more behind this facade.

Was I prepared to open that can of worms? Probably not.

7

VICTORIA

WE ARRIVED at Jack's building half an hour after I tucked Scarlett safely into her bed. The attendant opened the door to the lobby, revealing a gray carpet lying on top of a black-and-white marble floor and a crystal chandelier hanging from the ceiling.

"How are you tonight, Sam?" Jack asked the doorman.

I stood beside Jack, admiring Sam's uniform. A notch lapel jacket with contrasting trim on the sleeve, his pants had a matching gold stripe on the side. This building was *so* over the top. The best thing about my lobby was the day-old bagels they left at the desk. I meant, the small round table that the building manager sometimes did paperwork on. I had to remind myself that this would have been my life if my father had acknowledged me as his daughter. But then again, maybe I should be grateful instead for the woman I was, living off the money I earned instead of my family's wealth.

"Fine, Mr. Turner. I wanted to thank you for allowing my daughter, Beth, to come to your office for the day and shadow one of your paralegals."

"It's my pleasure. If that's the career choice Beth wants to make, tell her to work hard and get those high LSAT scores, so she'll be able to get into Harvard Law."

"I don't know if I could afford Harvard." Sam laughed nervously.

"When the time comes, tell her to come and see me. Brookman Farlow Turner Lit Law Firm also has grants for students like Beth."

"Thank you, Mr. Turner. That would be great." He shook Jack's hand.

With my mouth half-open, I followed Jack inside the elevator.

"Why are you looking at me like that?"

"Wow, the Tin Man has a heart," I murmured, standing next to him in the elevator.

"Tin Man?" He chuckled, pressing number fifteen on the panel. "You're mistaken. I have no desire to find my heart." He took a step closer. "What I do want is to back you into this corner and kiss you like you've never been before," he seductively whispered into my ear.

The heat rose from the back of my neck. "I know what you're doing. Stop distracting me with your advances, Jack," I said, pressing the button to the fifteenth floor nonstop like it would move the elevator faster. "Why would you do that for him if you didn't care?"

Jack let out a long breath before saying, "Do you know how hard it is to find a doorman as qualified as Sam? Sam is a second-generation doorman. His position was passed from his father." He casually slid his hands into his pockets and looked down at me. "I'm not doing him a favor; I'm doing myself a favor by keeping him happy."

Something in his eyes didn't have me buying it. Jack wasn't all he wanted everyone to perceive him to be—an insensitive jerk.

We stood next to each other in silence until the bell dinged.

We passed through the decorated hallway with paintings and purple flowers in a translucent vase sitting on the console table. He unlocked his door and gestured for me to go inside. His apartment was modern chic mixed with mid-century furniture. In the den was a poker table, a flat screen television, and a foosball table. I smiled. It was the ultimate bachelor pad. Then, Jack showed me the gigantic kitchen with two stoves, a massive island, and stainless steel appliances.

Why would a man need so much?

There was a staircase off to the side in the corridor that I assumed led to the bedrooms, undoubtedly decorated in the same fashion.

After Jack gave me the tour of the first floor, I sat down on the leather sofa that looked out to the terrace. The Manhattan skyline looked like an urban fairy tale, and the large patio door framed the beautiful view like art. The penthouse was silent; I heard nothing but peace. At my place, every night was filled with sirens and angry voices. I was so lost in my trance that I didn't notice Jack coming back into the room.

"Beautiful, right?" he asked, and I flinched.

I stared blankly while Jack strolled back to the couch, wearing sweatpants and a plain T-shirt.

"What the hell happened?" I asked. "Do you have a casual twin brother hidden back there or what?" I allowed my eyes to run the length of him.

The side of his mouth went up seductively. "Your cute you know that? I don't always wear a suit. I do like to get more comfortable when I get home."

"More comfortable than wearing jeans?" My eyes ran up and down the length of him. "I'm glad you're telling me this because, for a second, I thought I was here for a fashion show." I giggled.

"Sorry, not tonight, honey." A smile tugged at his lips. "Like the view?" he said, and I rolled my eyes. "I meant that." He nudges his head to the skyline.

"Yes, the view is extraordinary. But I see why you position the couch this way. I bet it's to woo your lady friends," I teased. My cheeks burned red, but some of that could have been from the alcohol.

"I don't have any lady friends." He chuckled. "You don't have to keep your guard up, Victoria. I get the message. Nothing's going to happen between us even if you beg me."

"That's absurd," I gasped. "Never in a lifetime would I beg you."

"That's what you say now." Jack looked smug while grabbing the only bottle of brownish-yellow alcohol from the small bar he had in the corner and poured two glasses. "Let's talk about the poker game." He walked back to me, holding two tumblers.

"I'm good, thanks."

"It's apple juice." He nudged the glass closer.

Scrunching my brows, I took it out of his hand and slowly sat up as I swirled the liquid in the glass. Sniffing it, I downed the liquid, loving its sweet taste.

"Why do you have apple juice in a whiskey decanter?" I flashed him an amused look.

"When I'm here with a woman, sometimes, she wants more alcohol. I know she can't handle any more, so I give her this, and she doesn't know the difference."

"What a gentleman." I snorted, prompting him to pour me more. I downed it again and placed the glass on the coffee table.

"You'd be surprised what drunk girls will believe."

"Ah," I said, slipping off my shoes, "so you're an enabler." I rested my arm on the top of the couch and pulled my legs closer in.

"I swear, I have never taken advantage of a woman. I just

follow along with the choices they make," Jack said, sitting down beside me.

I looked at him in disbelief. "You still manipulate them. You play the nonchalant card, but secretly, you still have one thing on your mind." I paused, thinking about what he'd told me that night I threw him into a cab. "But then again ... you haven't been with a woman in over a year?" I bobbed my head to the side.

"Why on earth did I tell you that?" he groaned, putting a hand through his hair.

"A year! Think about it; you're almost a virgin again," I said, laughing. "I'm curious though; is it by choice, or is it because you can't stick it up?"

He snapped his head back at me. "You're having way too much fun with this, aren't you?"

"So, it is a problem." My eyes widened in disbelief.

"It's not a problem. Do you want me to show you?" A wide, brilliant grin appeared on his face.

"No, thanks. I'll pass," I said even though I knew Jack was a *man* in all definition. I'd never dated a guy like Jack before. Confidence radiated off his perfect, toned body. I had to admit that desire wasn't the issue, but then I'd think of what he did for a living, and it was like throwing a bucket of ice-cold water over me.

"All right. If you ever change your mind ..." He shrugged playfully.

"Thanks for the offer, but it will never happen," I said, straightening my blouse without meeting his eyes.

There was a pause of silence before Jack said, "Look ... I went through something horrible a while back, and it left me in shambles." He turned to gaze at me. "And I ... didn't feel the same after that. Sex is just not a priority these days." He shrugged.

I saw something in his eyes, and it made me regret the way I was behaving. I'd forgotten that Jack, even though he was a lawyer, was still human, not immune to life's pain and struggles.

"I'm sorry, Jack. It wasn't nice of me to—"

"It's fine." He leveled me with a look. "I'm kidding. The whole apple juice thing—I haven't brought anyone up here in ages. The truth is, I have no alcohol in the house," he said. "I got rid of it all."

"Why did you get rid of it?" I shifted my body, leaning my chin into my hand.

"Because I'd been drinking a little too much lately." His eyes met mine before looking into his glass. "I didn't like how you looked at me the night that you put me into a cab, like you were disappointed. I barely know you, yet it affected me," he said, rotating with the glass in his hands. "Honestly, Victoria, whatever you think of me, the only intention I had that night was to make sure you got home safe, but instead, it was you who took care of me. I would never forgive myself if something had happened to you that night," he said, and his sincerity moved me.

"It's not the first time I traveled around the city by myself, Jack. I'm not yours to worry about," I said.

He looked at me before diverting his gaze back to the skyline. I loved to hate this man, and now he made me feel something else. I don't know what it was, but it wasn't hate.

"So, you're quitting cold turkey? By using apple juice?" I asked, because I was curious.

"Whatever works, right?" He smirked.

That was why, at the bar, all he'd had was a Perrier.

"Why didn't you say something? We could have gone somewhere else instead of that dingy bar."

"Aha! You did want to come out with me tonight. Nice touch though, using your friend to put a wedge between us."

"You like that one, hey?" I raised my brow. "You're not the only one who has aces up their sleeves."

"I don't need to play games, Victoria. I can't help if most women are just drawn to me." He smiled smugly.

Wow, our heart-to-heart moment didn't last long.

"You're arrogant." I cast him a look of disapproval.

"Or maybe that's what I want you to think." He winked, spreading his arms across the top of the couch. "You're not interested, so I can say whatever I want. This is another one of my plays though." He brushed his nails at the top of his shirt.

"I thought you said you didn't play games?" I narrowed my eyes at him.

"I make plays. There's a difference. This is a move that makes me that much more desirable to women, especially difficult ones," he said, and I snorted a laugh.

Boy, Jack Turner is sure entertaining.

"Like me, who you don't have a chance in hell with?" I chuckled. "Okay, hotshot, tell me more about this move. How does it play out?"

Jack cleared his throat and rolled up his invisible sleeves to look important. He sat back and turned, so our knees touched. "I'd talk you up about your career goals and all the things you wished you could have done in your life."

"Interesting." I arched my brows in amusement.

"After you answered, I'd tell you about my work, and you'd pretend like you hadn't been Googling my cases the whole time. Then, I'd do the line."

"Of course there's a line," I said with an eye roll. "All right." I take a deep breath before letting it out. "Okay, I'm ready. Bring it on." I flashed him a sarcastic smile.

He grabbed both my hands and looked deep into my eyes, and at first, it felt like we were having a moment, but then I had to remind myself that this was Jack.

"Victoria, at the end of the day, I just want to be a regular guy. I don't need fancy clothes or cars. I just need you and me tonight."

"Oh, please," I groaned, snatching my hands back.

"No, that is the exact reaction the line always gets. Then, I pair it with the proof of changing into this, and—*bang*—you're all over me."

I shook my head and rubbed my tired eyes. "You're insane. What do your clothes prove? No wonder you haven't had sex in over a year!" I let out a laugh.

"That I'm not materialistic and I can be vulnerable with you in my basic clothes."

"Oh God."

"That's what they say, too, but later." He winked.

"You're an egotistical pig," I huffed, putting my shoes back on.

"You're not leaving yet, are you?"

"I think I've seen enough from the great Jack Turner," I said, picking up my purse from the coffee table.

"What about the poker night?"

"Are we actually going to talk about that?" I gave him a flat look.

He nodded. "That's why I brought you here. You're the one who was interested in my moves."

I chewed my lower lip as I settled back on the couch, wondering why I wasn't being honest with myself. I was in trouble if I ever viewed Jack Turner as more than a hotshot attorney. I just had to find a way to keep it like that. Then, I thought about Jack's firm and how they'd screwed my mother and my life. The way Jack might have done to someone else, and my feelings for Jack—dislike—were right on track. This was business and nothing more. *So I told myself.*

8

JACK

"YOU SAID EVERYTHING WAS MY CALL." Victoria tilted her head to the side.

"It is. I'll even give you my credit card."

"It's fine. I'll put everything on mine and send you the bill later."

"Are you sure?"

"Yeah." She shrugged like I'd offended her. "I can send you a draft of the menu by tomorrow, and I know how to talk to your type of crowd. Be super sweet, bat my eyelashes, and pretend they have a shot with me to get more tips. And, whatever I earn in tips, I will donate it to your cause—that is, I would need to know more about it first." She smiled.

She was conniving like me, though she would never admit it.

"I like where your head is at." I grinned. "You can choose anything for the menu and any decor items you think I might need." My eyes dragged around the room before they landed back on her. "I do, however, need to know you can play on their heartstrings. These guys have wives and children, but I don't think they've experienced true loss. They need to know the importance of their investments and what my charity can do for sick kids."

"How can I do that?" Victoria asked.

"Tell them a story. Has there ever been a time when you wished you could have done more for someone and you missed your chance? That's exactly the story we would need to tell them."

"You want me to sound like an infomercial?" she quipped. "And what makes your charity so special? Why should they even think of signing a check over to you?"

I smiled.

"What?" she asked, arms folded.

"I knew you would say that."

"And that's good?" She raised her brows.

"It's perfect!" I poured another round of juice for us and then drank mine. "These are the exact questions the guys are going to ask, and I need you to answer them. They're more likely to listen to an intelligent woman like you than their attorney buddy."

"What if they think you hired me to talk them up?" Her eyes met mine for a brief second before diverting to the coffee table. She leaned over, picking her glass up.

"I'll be up-front about that. They'll know you're catering, but they won't know that I've planted you there to tell your story. Have you thought of anything?" I asked.

"Yes," she said before throwing back the glass like it was smooth liquor.

"Can I hear it?"

"No." Her eyes darted, not allowing me to see what was in them.

"Why not?" I asked, watching her get up.

"I can't talk about it. Not when it's just you and me. I'll do it in a room full of people where I can pretend it's just an act.

That's what you want right? An act?" she said over her shoulder as she marched out onto the terrace.

What the heck just happened?

I observed Victoria through the patio door as the wind flowed through her chestnut silky hair. I got up, grabbing a gray blanket off the couch, and made my way toward the exit. At the other end of the gallery, Victoria stood there, rubbing her arms, peering down at the busy streets. Without making a big deal about it, I came from behind and wrapped a blanket over her shoulders.

"I don't want it," she said, throwing it off.

"Stop being so stubborn." Before she said another word, I enveloped her inside the soft threads and rested my hands against the railing. "I need your help, Victoria," I pleaded. "I need you to tell your story, and it needs to sound genuine, so I can convince my friends to donate their money."

"I thought you wanted to hire a caterer," she challenged, pulling the gray cover tighter around her before shuffling away until she reached the brick wall.

"I do. I just thought, since you'd done volunteer work at the clinic, you'd be interested in helping me out."

"How did you know that?" Her eyes widened.

"Know what?" I shrugged.

"Who told you I used to volunteer at the hospital?"

"Well, I ..."

The first time I had seen Victoria was by the elevator doors at the children's hospital, wearing those tags around her neck—the ones that volunteers wore. But then I would have to explain what I was doing there at the hospital, and I wasn't ready to talk about that just yet.

"I had a feeling you did," I answered finally, but the look on her face made me think she didn't believe me.

"Tell me yours, and I'll tell you mine."

"My what?" I glanced at her.

"Your story. Why are you starting this charity?" Victoria asked.

"I don't have one," I lied, stepping away. I walked to the opposite side of the terrace. "I told you already. I'm just doing this for my friends."

"Why do I feel like there's more to the story?" Her dark eyes flit over me.

Victoria was an intelligent woman who didn't like to be taken for a ride. She deserved the truth, and I wanted to give it to her, but if I told her my situation, she would think I was no better than her father. What kind of man wanted a woman to look at him like he was a coward? Because that was what she'd do.

"I had a friend who was very sick ... I made a promise to him before he died that I would do more good things with my time and money, and this is one of those things. Whatever we make that night, I'm planning on matching it," I told the only truth I was ready to disclose.

"Well, that was vague, but I'll accept it, I guess," she said, finally satisfied with my answer.

"Your turn."

Victoria bit her lip before speaking, "My younger half-brother Chris"—she swallowed—"he had cancer. He lived in and out of hospitals his whole life, so I know how important money is when there is a sick child in the family."

My stomach tightened. "How is he doing now?"

"He's not ... he died ten years ago," she said and then abruptly entered the living room.

When she realized I was right behind her, she continued going. I followed her as she made her way into the kitchen.

Why did she keep trying to get away from me?

"I'm sorry, Victoria," I said, catching up and pulling her into my arms. When I did, her body went still. "I'm sorry you had to go through something like that."

"Please, Jack, I don't want your pity," she said, tears shimmering in her eyes. "That's life. You have to deal with what comes your way." She walked out of my embrace to stand on the other side of the marble kitchen island.

Come back.

"I didn't mean to push you ... I had no idea." I rubbed the back of my neck. "I just ... want to get to know you better."

"I don't understand why." Her eyes softened, and I felt something go through me.

I had my own selfish reasons for wanting Victoria to open up to me. I needed her to talk about her family— especially about her mother.

"What's not to understand? You're smart, beautiful ... you're not the woman of my dreams," I said.

Victoria gave me a flat look, crossing her arms in front of her chest. And it makes me smile. She cared what I thought of her. I knew she did.

"That's because I never had one, but if I did, you'd be it." I inched my way closer to her. "You make me want to dream about love again."

My eyes took her in and I completely forgot what I had set out to do tonight. That was to get information out of her so I could use it in court against her mother. This was a moment of weakness, but around Victoria, I didn't know even how to breathe. That was the thing about her; she had no idea she had this power to crumble everything I'd built around me, around my heart.

"That's a good line." She smirked.

Didn't she believe me? Here I was, making a fool of myself, and she was having none of it.

"I thought it was romantic." I shrugged.

"Romantic? If you were a divorce lawyer, then I would have found it ironic," she said with a wink.

There was that jab at the lawyer thing again.

This woman never ceases to amaze me.

"Okay, why don't you tell me why you hate lawyers so much?" I asked when I got close enough.

Then I couldn't help myself from brushing the hair from her face.

"Who was the one to break your heart?" she threw back.

My stomach twisted at the thought of Colleen. She was a woman I dated back at Harvard were we both were law students. She was everything I wanted in a woman, smart, strong and ambitious so much so I was getting in her way. Colleen dictated everything in our relationship. She wanted her career and all I wanted was her. We never saw eye to eye on anything so we broke up. She did come back to me eventually, and allowing her into my life again was the biggest mistake. Colleen broke my heart again, only this time there was no coming back from it.

There was no way in hell I was going to have this conversation with Victoria.

"I asked you first," I said.

She huffed. "I don't hate lawyers, more like your firm, and you ... well, you just rub me the wrong way."

"Do I?" I smiled in amusement.

"You really do have one thing on your mind." She smacked my hand away from playing with her long strands of hair.

"Woman, cut me some slack. It's been a while. Besides, you walked in on that one all on your own." I flashed a grin. "So, tell me about this lawyer who broke your heart."

She snorted. "As if. I would never in a million years date a lawyer."

"So, what is it then?"

"I don't want to get into it." She waved me away and marched out of the room.

I never thought I would say this, but it was getting exhausting, chasing her around in my apartment. I made a mental note to buy duct tape.

"Why not? I bared my soul to you."

"Bared your soul?" She spun around. "Ever since we met, you've told me minor details here and there that don't really amount to anything. You don't want me to know your secrets, the ones that you don't tell anyone because then you'll lose the power. The things that make you a real human." Victoria sat back down on the couch.

I sat on the armrest. "What have you done to deserve to know my secrets?"

She pondered my question, which had some value to it.

"You've been rude to me for the majority of our interactions, and I didn't let your friend or you pay for the drinks tonight. Don't you think I deserve to know?" I asked.

"I'll tell you. How's that?" She let out a long breath.

"Now, we're getting somewhere," I said, knocking her feet off the coffee table to sit down beside her. "Let's have it. Tell me all your darkest secrets, Victoria." I cast her a look of amusement.

"I think the only mystery here is you, hotshot. I don't think Scar even knows about this, so you should feel honored that I'm telling you."

"I know how to spot a stall when I see one. Bullshit, you tell your best friend everything," I told her.

"Okay, fine." Victoria nervously brushed her hair from her face. "Up until I was a teenager, I didn't know who my father was. For the longest time, my mother told me that he was a one-night stand. She didn't know his name and barely remembered what he looked like."

"Is this your mom's secret or yours?" I furrowed my brows.

"Do you want to know why I hate your firm or not?" She glared at me, and I gestured for her to continue. "Then, when I was sixteen, I found this shoebox full of pictures and article clippings. I read about Arthur Fairfax, my grandfather, and saw pictures of my mother and father's elopement in the newspaper clippings. When I asked my mom about it, she told me her marriage was a Vegas sham, and he had already been engaged to someone else. My father abandoned us before I was born because he was going to be cut off from his father's fortune. It's clear who he chose," she said.

My heart faltered. I wished I could tell her what I knew about her parents, but then I would be breaking lawyer-client confidentiality. She took a quick glance in my direction, and I felt my pressure drop.

"Are you okay?" Her eyes filled with concern.

I cleared my throat. "Yeah, sure, um ... continue."

Her eyes dragged across my face before she said, "I was told by my mother that, after a DNA paternity test was done, my father publicly denied being my father, and a legal case followed, but your firm made sure that everything would go away and that my mother and I wouldn't get a cent from my father." She shrugged.

DNA? Publicly denied being her father? I didn't remember seeing that in the files.

"He wanted nothing to do with me. His name is the only thing he could give me, and that wasn't even voluntary."

Something was not right here, and I felt a peg at the bottom of my stomach. Her mother was either a big, fat liar or my client was.

"He has two kids, both a few years younger than me. I haven't Googled him in a while, but I know my grandfather survived a stroke recently, and George, my father, lives off of his father's money."

"That sounds tough, Victoria. I can't imagine that was easy to go through."

"No, it wasn't, but I've been dealing with it my whole life." She shrugged, and I handed her a box of tissues. "I'm not crying."

"Could it be a delayed reaction?" I said.

She tossed the box at me, and I chuckled. *Such venom! God, she was a stunner.*

Never had I met a woman who turned me on so badly. She was probably the one to break the dry spell. It was a shame I'd never find out.

"What's going on with the poker night? How long do I have to plan it?"

Sitting up straight, I cleared my throat. "Next weekend. I'll leave a key at the desk for you, so you can come early. I'm expecting everyone by eight. Plan accordingly."

"I'll send you an invoice by e-mail," Victoria said, brushing herself off and straightening her clothes.

"You leaving?"

"Yes, it's getting late," she said as I sat there, looking up at her, wishing she wouldn't go.

I knew she wasn't the type to have flings, and no matter what she was accusing me of, I really just wanted to get to know her. I enjoyed talking to her, and tonight, in my apartment, it didn't seem so lonely. Something about Victoria concerned me about getting involved with her professionally, but I smothered those voices out of my head.

"Are you really taking Scarlett to the function next Saturday?"

I hated how she kept using Scarlett like a partition. I knew she did it because she was scared, but so was I, which was all the more reason we should be together. But I didn't tell her that.

"I'd rather take you. The offer is still on the table."

"No," she said with a hint of disappointment on her face. "Scarlett seems to have her heart set on going. But don't you dare take advantage of her," she added.

"I wouldn't do that," I said honestly. "There's something you should know about me, Victoria. When I give someone my word, I am good for it."

She nodded.

Another event, another woman that I dreaded dangling from my arm. *What would it take for Victoria to trust me?* Someone was going to get hurt, and my gut feeling told me that this situation was about to get ugly.

"I'm going to drive you home. Ready to go?" I asked.

9

VICTORIA

IT WAS a beautiful day on the outside, but inside, I was experiencing a thunderstorm. I called Scarlett a hundred times. She hadn't come home last night, which only meant she might have spent the night at Jack's place, but it wasn't like her not to call.

I went to work in the morning to help set up for the afternoon venue, thinking she would show up to tell me about her night, as we always memorized each other's schedules. Walking around with a silver tray, I offered people drinks and hors d'oeuvres, most of them not caring it was too early to dress like they were Cinderella at a ball.

The event took place in a Georgian town mansion that had a pedigree legacy attached to it. The decor was very Victorian, the rooms filled with heavy drapes and antique vases. A sweeping staircase was next to the thirty-two-foot drawing room with a view of the beautiful gardens. Inside the garage housed several luxury cars. I knew because the owner was extremely proud to show them off to the staff of Florence Catering.

I imagined Jack would love to live in a place like this, and I'd bet he owned a home in the Hamptons where he took his more serious love interests ... maybe even Scarlett one day. I couldn't take him and Scarlett off my mind, regularly checking my phone to see if she had called.

The night before, she had gone with Jack as his date for a function he had, and when she hadn't come home, I couldn't sleep the whole night. I guessed Jack had fixed his problem. Why was it bothering me? They were adults. It was none of my business what they did. I wasn't envious. Why would I be? Jack had invited me first. He'd wanted me to go with him instead of Scarlett, but I would never tell her that she was the consolation prize. And, for some strange reason, I was content, knowing that fact. I loved Scarlett, but sometimes, I felt like she was always in competition with me when it came to men. She had to be the center of attention, and I never minded that—until now.

Why hadn't she called me yet? Was she passed out somewhere? What wild adventure was she pushing him into? Or vice versa? I felt like her mother, angry that she was out past her curfew. I knew Jack was many things, but he wouldn't take advantage of her—that he'd promised. I was dying to call the number Jack had given me to keep in touch with him for the poker night I was planning for him, but then it would look like I was checking up on him.

On my break, I slipped away to the restroom down in the basement, which had a Japanese inspired wallpaper and a gold-framed mirror. Locking the door, I called Scarlett again and straightened out my bow tie. On the last ring, Scarlett picked up.

"Hello?" she said, sounding like she'd just woken up.

"Scarlett, where have you been?" I hissed.

"Mom?"

"No, it's Victoria."

"Victoria who?"

She was testing my patience. I brought down the lid of the toilet and plopped down.

"Hilarious, Scarlett," I huffed.

"I'm kidding. What's the problem?" Scarlett's voice came out groggy. There was no sound in the background, and I was guessing she was alone, but I felt uneasy to ask her.

"Where the hell have you been?" I asked, controlling the tension in my voice.

No matter what I felt, I focused on the fact she was okay and that was all that mattered.

"Sleeping," she said.

Suddenly, the walls in the tiny restroom felt like they were closing in. She could have been sleeping alone, away from Jack, right? Just because she'd spent the night over didn't mean something had happened between them.

"You were supposed to call when you were on your way home from the party, and you never did."

"That's so sweet you were worried about me, but I was in good hands," she said, and my stomach twisted in knots.

Sure she was.

"I'll be home later." She giggled.

"I thought you were working today?"

"I traded shifts with Eva," she continued. "I'll tell you all about my night when I see you, okay? And believe me, there is a lot to tell. A. Lot."

I hated the fact that she was trying to rub it in my face. Well, I guessed Jack had had no trouble last night, and Scarlett was the right antidote.

"Okay, I get it. See you later." I hung up, and then my phone beeped with a winking face emoji sent by Scarlett.

Stuffing my phone in my pocket, I went back out to the party. I did my best to keep smiling, but the only thought on my mind was Scarlett's safety.

From myself.

I almost snapped at a party guest and had to go home early because my boss said I was upsetting the guests.

What on earth was going on with me?

LATER, I entered our apartment, and I called out for Scarlett even though I knew she wasn't home yet. After making dinner, I went to my room to read my romance novel, but then I wasn't in the mood for that, so I picked up a thriller instead about a woman who murdered her boyfriend.

That's better.

It wasn't until eight p.m. that I heard the key in the lock. Jumping out of bed, I rushed to the door to see Scarlett wearing a baggy T-shirt and sweatpants.

"Are those Jack's clothes?" I asked, trying not to sound like a jealous boyfriend.

"Yes!" she squealed, running toward me for a hug.

She swung me around, and I remained rigid.

"What the hell happened to you? I was worried sick."

Scarlett went to the kitchen to pour us each a glass of wine. She placed them on the coffee table and then pulled me down to the couch. "I had the most amazing night."

"And not to mention, day." I scrunched my nose and took a swig of wine. "With Jack?" I swallowed but it lodged in my throat. I only had myself to blame.

"Who else?" she said, playfully swatting my arm. She hugged a throw pillow, and the smile on her face never faded. "He is such an attentive person. It's like he knows everything I want before I ask for it."

I bet Jack was very mindful of Scarlett's every whim if he knew he was getting something out of it. Jealous or not, I didn't need her to paint me a picture of the wild night they had together.

"Ew, can you skip to the part where you were coming home?"

"You're such a prude," she said. "Relax, he's such a gentleman. After the party, we went back to his place and spent most of the night talking until I fell asleep on his couch."

My eyes widened. "You mean, nothing happened?" I asked.

But she talked over me, as usual, "He's such a worldly man, and he knows practically every rich person in New York. He's sophisticated, and he can talk about art and culture. He even taught me a few tricks he uses in the courtroom, but I'm sworn to secrecy. Jack let me stay in his apartment as long as I wanted."

What a gentleman.

"And where was he?" I asked, trying to sound unaffected.

"When I woke up, breakfast was made, and he'd left me a note saying he had work to do at the office. I didn't want to go home in an uncomfortable dress, so I allowed myself to borrow his clothes. He smells so good!" Scarlett brings the sleeve to her nose.

"What did you guys talk about?" I asked, taking a sip out of my glass.

"We talked about everything. Even about you." She gave me a side-glance.

"Me?" Something inside me lit up. "What about?"

"He asked about your mother and father."

That was strange. *Why would Jack be interested in my parents?*

"And what did you tell him?" I asked her.

"I told him the truth—that you never talk about them, and I know nothing,"

What was Jack up to? Lawyers always worked on angles, and I wondered what kind of angle he had on me.

"I think we have a true connection. This could turn into something real."

Her eyes lit up, and my stomach twisted, even more so since I knew I was the reason all this was happening. I should have never brought her with me that night.

"He's a player, Scar. What's real about that? That's all there is to it." I shrugged.

She snuggled closer, smelling like cologne. Jack's cologne.

Don't tell me she's fallen for him. I didn't think I'd ever seen Scarlett so carried away. She'd only known him twenty-nine hours, and eight hours had been spent sleeping—hopefully in separate rooms. Far separate rooms, preferably under different roofs.

Great, I have turned into the green-eyed monster. Why couldn't I be happy for her?

I tightly hugged her and rested my chin on the top of her head.

"I know I promised you I wouldn't talk about him, but he's unlike any man I've ever met. Everyone I've been with is a child compared to him. They wouldn't know sophistication if it bit them in the ass," Scarlett said.

"That's what you get from men in their twenties, Scar, especially at the places you pick them up. You've only dated party-goers and bad boys. You've never been with someone who has a real career and plenty of life experience. I'm surprised it hasn't scared you away."

"That's what makes him so special. I'm comfortable around him. He makes me feel sophisticated, and he doesn't talk down to me like a lot of the men we work with do. He's an incredible guy, and I can't wait to see him again."

Yep, that's Jack for you. He made himself so irresistible to women, and it would only be a matter of time he would get bored with Scarlett and move on to the next one.

"You're seeing him again?" I pulled away to get a better look at her.

"Yeah, I wrote him a note on his bathroom mirror with my red lipstick, saying that I wanted to meet up later," she said, snuggling her head into my chest, and I found myself very annoyed.

I frowned. "Are you sure that's a good idea?"

Scarlett sat up and bopped my nose. "You're cute when you worry, but Jack is one of the good ones."

"How do you know?" I could answer that question if only I wasn't such a prude and I gave Jack a chance.

"I can just tell."

I cleared my throat. "Don't get too invested. Jack is not boyfriend material."

I was an awful friend. *Why was I trying to sabotage this?* Deep down, I knew Jack was not for her.

But was he for me?

What was I going to do with my unresolved feelings for Jack?

"Maybe right now, but who knows what will happen?" Scarlett shrugged and then twirled around as she stood and stretched.

"I'm going to get ready for bed," Scarlett said.

"Yeah, sure. I'm kind of tired too."

She ran to the bathroom to take a shower. And, as I sat there, listening to Scarlett singing at the top of her lungs, I wanted to hide under a rock and never come out.

I went to my room and curled up in bed. This was how it always started. She'd find a guy that I liked and instantly jump to the end of their story, which ended in self-destruction. Either way, I had to mind my own business and just pick up the pieces when the time came. Only who would pick up mine?

10

VICTORIA

FOR THE NEXT WEEK, I took a few extra catering jobs to keep myself busy. I didn't know what was going on between Scarlett and Jack, nor did I care. I just didn't want to be around to witness anything.

Out of sight, out of mind.

Also, I was too busy planning the menu for Jack's poker night. I had a feeling these men wouldn't be picky as long as I chose the right kind of beer and food. That would be the starting point, and then I would introduce the harder stuff before I gave them my speech about why it was important to invest in the charity. That way, they wouldn't notice how nervous I was. Even though I had everything written, it didn't make me feel any better.

How could I speak without breaking down? Telling a story I'd been trying to cope with for years wasn't easy to do.

One of such tragic proportions.

I knew my words would become jumbled if I didn't practice in the mirror. I needed to get it right, so they could donate their money for a good cause that would help kids like Luke and Chris. If I rushed out of Jack's house in a panic, I probably wouldn't get paid. Money and telling the story correctly were my only focus. Jack had promised me I would make tips on top of what he paid me. He would also share my business card with them, so I could do more independent catering jobs. Who knew? Maybe this would be the start of something good.

I rushed into my living room, pulling on my blazer and running over my checklist before I peered over at Scarlett, who was sitting on the couch.

"Where are your keys? I need to pick everything up on the way to Jack's place," I said.

"Oh, you don't need my car tonight."

Scarlett shot up from the sofa, taking my notepad from my hands and tossing it into the air. I snatched it back before she could catch it.

"Why not?" I asked.

"Jack said he'd send his driver to pick you up. Isn't that so kind of him? He's always thinking of other people. Money is no object to him. He's a perfect man, striving to make the world better."

She was making me nauseous. *What was the matter with her these days? It couldn't be love, could it?* But it felt more like she was rubbing it in my face.

"One luxury vehicle at a time," I huffed, throwing around clothes and pizza boxes to find my wallet.

Heaven's sake, I needed a place of my own.

"Exactly! Who said money can't buy happiness?" Scarlett grinned.

"But how do you know he sent a driver?" I stopped to glance back at her.

"He called on your cell phone while you were in the shower," she said.

I regarded her for a moment. *Why would she be picking up my phone? Hadn't she and Jack been in contact this whole time?*

"Oh, anyway, I don't want to take a driver. I can drive myself. It's not like I'm going to be drinking," I said, grabbing my purse. No luck. My wallet was not there either.

"You can't say no to him. I bet his driver is already on the way. Are you sure I can't come?" Scarlett emerged from her room and handed me my wallet.

"What was it doing in there?" I asked, my eyes meeting hers.

The past few weeks, this had been becoming a habit with Scarlett. If she needed money, I wished she would come out and say so instead of stealing it from me.

"What is anything doing here? We live in a pigsty." Her eyelids dropped.

"We wouldn't if you knew how to tidy up!" I growled. I leaned against the kitchen counter and made sure everything was still inside, but it wasn't.

"I didn't steal anything."

"I know you didn't," I said even though there was a twenty-dollar bill missing. "One of your late flings might have," I murmured. I only let her get away with it because she allowed me to borrow her car.

"I haven't slept with anyone since I met Jack." She smiled proudly.

"What's going on with you two?" I arched my brow.

She hadn't seen Jack lately ... not that I knew of.

"We're taking it slow." She shrugged.

I'd noticed in the last few weeks that she wouldn't talk about him unless I brought him up professionally, and even though I had been in contact with Jack, we never spoke about Scarlett. If they weren't seeing each other, why didn't she just say so instead of being so secretive about it?

I watched her walk to the kitchen and open a bag of potato

chips. "I want Jack," she said. "And I'm going to be with him whether you like it or not. Unless you're jealous of us?"

I scoffed and shook my head. "No, I'm just trying to look out for you, Scar. If he hurts you in any way and I could have done something to stop it, I would never forgive myself," I said.

No matter what I felt about Jack, it didn't overshadow the fact that I didn't want to see Scarlett get hurt. I took a chip from the bag, and Scarlett hugged me, crushing it between us.

"I know you're worried about me, but heartbreak is a part of love. No matter what, I'll be okay, but I know Jack cares about me."

Oh brother.

"Okay," I said, pulling away, and when I did, my jacket was all greasy. "Scarlett," I huffed.

"Did I do that? Oops. Sorry." She popped another chip in her mouth, chewing it slowly.

Something in her face made me believe it had been intentional. But I had no time to call her out on it, I was already running late.

"I have to go." I rushed to my room and pulled my jean jacket out of the closet.

"If you need anything, call me," Scarlett said as I marched to the front door.

"Later!" I shouted and then left the apartment.

WHEN I ENTERED Jack's place, it was silent, eerie almost. I stocked the bar and organized the food in the fridge. Then, I had an hour to kill before the guests would show. Jack wasn't there, or if he was, he didn't come out of hiding. I strolled around the room, wearing a black dress and flats. Jack wanted me to dress sexy, and this was as good as it would get. I didn't need to flirt with these men to convince them the charity was worth it—or at least, I hoped not.

Circling the poker table, I ran my fingers along the chips and imagined what it would be like to play this game in Vegas. I'd never been there, but my mother and her boyfriend went there often, and they always won quite a bit of money. I was never the gambling type, but trying to understand the thrill of it might be a far stretch. Sitting in a leather chair, I pretended to hold the playing cards. I didn't want to unwrap a new deck and mess up anything for the dealer Jack had hired.

As I leaned back in my seat, my eyes caught something in the dark mahogany bookshelf. I got up and went across the room. Jack had personal mementos, maybe things he'd gotten from his trips, pictures of family and friends. But what interested me was a picture of Jack and a boy in a baseball cap. As I got closer to the picture frame, a noise from behind startled me and caused me to knock down a ceramic vase with my elbow.

Shoot.

My heart skipped a beat as I checked to make sure there was no other damage besides the porcelain vase, and then I pushed the shattered pieces with my shoe under the table until I could find something to pick it up with.

"Don't worry; it's not worth anything," Jack said, appearing at the top of the stairs.

"Jack." My cheeks burned red. "I didn't know you were here."

This is embarrassing.

"I had a couple of conference calls to attend to," he said, descending the stairs. "I thought I'd heard you come in. You should have said hi."

"Sam said you were out." I peered at the floor, scuffing my feet. "I didn't expect you until the game started."

"No, he was mistaken."

"I'm sorry I broke your vase." I lifted my hands in defeat.

"And you tried to hide it." He chuckled.

"I, um ... I panicked." I laughed nervously. "I'll pay for the damages."

"Don't worry about it. You did me a favor; I never liked that ugly thing anyway."

"The least I can do is clean it up. Where do you keep your broom?" I bent down to pick up the larger pieces.

"Leave it there. I'll take care of it later."

He leaned closer and took my wrist, which forced me to look up at him. Jack was dressed in a fitted blue shirt with the sleeves rolled up, paired with black pants. He smelled clean, delicious. *Sandalwood?*

"While we have the time, why don't you help me pick out the music for tonight?" He walked to a cabinet beside his television and opened it to reveal a high-tech stereo system. "I had someone install speakers throughout the apartment, so I get the perfect surround-sound experience. Helen, my secretary, set me up with this IT expert, and he synced everything up to my phone. Cool, right?"

"Nowadays, everything happens on the phone, so it's not that impressive," I teased, pouring myself a glass of apple juice at his bar, and then I slipped back into the seat at the poker table. "Are you going to be okay with all this alcohol around?" I asked, knowing this was something we should have discussed beforehand.

"It won't be easy, but when I put my mind to something, I kind of stick to it," Jack said, and I believed him.

It was not always easy, resisting temptation, and cocktails were part of the menu. But I could see it in Jack's eyes that he was determined, and I admired him for it.

"You play?" Jack asked, nodding toward the table.

"Blackjack is more my thing," I said, fiddling with a few poker chips. "It was the easiest one to learn. I have an uncle who lives on the West Coast, and he taught me everything I know. It crushed me to discover that he's a terrible gambler. Lost millions at the racetrack once."

"That's why I never bet on games that are pure chance," he said, pushing buttons on the remote for the entertainment system. "With poker, I feel like I have full control. I can look my opponent in the eye and know exactly what he's thinking. You have to be cunning, skilled, and understand the odds of success."

As he said this, I had to wonder if there was more to Jack than the lawyer in him. *Did he ever let his guard down? And why was it up in the first place?* Whatever it was must have been something traumatic.

"It's all about luck," I added. "If you don't have the right cards, you're done."

"Victoria, even if you have the worst hand in the game, it's possible to bluff your way through it. Only someone like me can succeed in that."

He was so smug, and yet I couldn't deny my attraction to him. Must be the apple juice. I peered down at my glass.

It has to be.

"Of course, because you're good at bluffing."

His mouth curved up. "Don't you dare say it, or I swear, Victoria ..."

Suddenly, I felt this conversation wasn't about a game of poker but a match between Jack and me. I wasn't ready to lay my cards on the table unless I knew what I was up against or if he was playing with Scarlett.

"Swear what?" I said as his gaze locked on mine.

"Keep on pushing my buttons with this lawyer bit, and you'll leave me no choice but to kiss you."

"Is that a threat?" I smirked, knowing that I shouldn't push it.

"Take it as you wish." A playful smile tugged at his lips.

For a second—*a very long second*—I considered what it would be like to kiss Jack. Hot and steamy, I'd bet. And, when my eyes found him staring back, the heat I was trying to contain, deep, deep down in the pit of my stomach washed over me, causing me to look like fifty shades of lobster red.

Ugh. Put a fork in it. I'm ready.

"Are we going to have music anytime soon?" I cleared my throat, making a quick decision to direct the conversation elsewhere.

Far away from our lips.

He was smiling, the kind when a man knew he had you just where he wanted you. This was Jack's ploy—planting a seed. Saying things just to rev up something inside of me, and obviously, it would work. I couldn't help it; I was human. Any woman in my position would fantasize about Jack Turner. Of course, that was what he wanted. But I could shut those ideas down and him out. All I had to do was think about Mr. Furley, ascots and all.

I shuddered. Yep, that should do it.

Last month, Scarlett and I got hooked on watching episodes of *Three's Company* on YouTube. I never thought it would be useful until now.

"What?"

"Play something, will you?" I smoothed out my hair and pretended like Jack wasn't watching me. When I glanced back up again, I was relieved to find Jack fiddling with the remote.

He pressed another button, and loud, piercing music blared from the stereo, shaking the entire apartment. I shouted at him, but Jack kept playing with the buttons to turn it off. When silence came, my ears buzzed, and I laughed at him.

"I think I pushed the wrong thing," Jack said, rubbing the back of his neck.

"You think?" I said, shouting louder than necessary. I walked over to the stereo to stand beside him. "I don't think rock music is the way to go."

"Why not?"

I flashed him a look. "Have you ever hosted a poker game before?"

"Have you?"

"Don't answer a question with a question," I said.

"I've hosted many poker games ..." he said hesitantly. "All right, this is my first."

"I thought so. Isn't that why I'm here?" I smiled, holding out my hands open to the side. I stepped closer and took the remote control out of his hand, pretending that his skin touching mine had no effect on me.

"You're going to want something more relaxed, smooth, like jazz. It has to be background music, not so overpowering that your guests can barely hear themselves think."

"I didn't mean to turn it up that loud." He chuckled.

"I'm sure you didn't." I giggled, studying the complicated controller. After a few minutes, I found a radio station with a relaxing mixture of easy rock and modern renditions of classical music. "There," I said, smiling. I walked back to the table, swaying to the music.

Jack grabbed my hand and pulled me into him. Suddenly, we were dancing, and I had my head on his chest.

What am I doing?

"I wanted to tell you before ... you look beautiful." He spun me outward and then drew me back in, our bodies pressed up against each other. I wanted to push him away, but we moved together so effortlessly that it felt right. "And I want to thank you for helping me out. You're going to bring a special touch tonight," he said, and I melted.

"You're paying me, so I have to do a good job," I said honestly.

"I think you would do a good job regardless. You're the type to go miles out of your way just to do a selfless act. In my line of work, you don't find that. Most of my clients are guilty of working the system. They don't do anything without getting something in return."

"Isn't everyone like that?" I asked, trying to push away, but he spun me around and then pulled me back to him.

His warm, muscular body caressed mine—

Mr. Furley.

"No, not you. I've never met someone like you before," Jack said as we stared in each other's eyes, and his arms tightened around my waist.

It had become too much for me that I was the one to break away from his gaze because I couldn't allow myself the liberty of being swept away in this moment. From my experience, men like Jack—wealthy, powerful, so self-assured—could only break your heart. I should know; that was what my father had done to my mother. He'd left her when she needed him most. And then there was something else—or I should say, someone else.

Scarlett.

"Jack, I ... I have to prepare stuff ... before the guests arrive," I said, breaking away.

I went to the kitchen and reorganized things to look like I was doing something and not trying to avoid Jack. I was doing my best to push him away, knowing we would never be right for each other. For one, I knew I was dealing with a whole load of issues. Abandonment was one of them. All I needed was for someone else to walk away from me, and Jack would most likely do that. And there was Scarlett. How could I do this to her? The last thing I should think about was kissing Jack Turner.

Mr. Furley. Mr. Furley.

"What can I do to help?"

I jumped at the sound of his voice and watched Jack stroll further into the kitchen.

"Nothing. I've got everything under control." Except for my feelings for Jack.

I rushed to the fridge and grabbed a beer and popped the cap. "Drink. It'll help your nerves." Then, I realized, *What the hell am I doing? Jack quit drinking.* "Shoot. Sorry, I forgot," I said, taking a big gulp.

"What nerves?" Jack tilted his head and sat down on a black leather stool at the white marble island.

"Your knee is shaking, and your palms are sweaty." I had taken note of it while we were dancing. Or was it my hands? "If that's not nerves, then what is it?" I grabbed a dish towel from one drawer and dabbed his forehead with it.

"That's because you're making me nervous," he said, dragging his eyes across my face in a way that was making me feel the heat from the back of my neck. His hand instinctively went to my waist, inching me closer.

Ascots and flashy-colored clothing. Focus, Victoria.

"It's not me that's doing this to you." I frowned, hating that he was saying all this stuff and making me feel things I didn't want to. "This is an important night," I said.

Jack's eyes lit up. "See? Right there. You did it again."

"What?" I asked, dropping my arms to the sides.

"You're helping me for no reason." His eyes trailed to my lips.

"I help when needed. It's part of my leadership skills. Why do you think I'm acting like this? I want you to refer me to every one of your fancy friends, remember?" I turned within his grasp, folding the dish towel on the counter, trying to ignore the fact that his hand was still on my waist. "Besides, you're my employer. I need you at your best."

"You want my night to go well because you care about me."

I gaped sarcastically. "Don't flatter yourself, Jack. I care about getting paid, so I can start my own business someday. You're a means to an end, and I don't need you thinking that I'm some saint who lives in a perfect little world."

"No, I wouldn't call you a saint." His eyes narrowed in thought. "I'm hoping there's some naughtiness somewhere inside you." He grinned.

"Wouldn't you like to know?" I bit the inside of my cheek. *What is wrong with me?*

I was flirting with him and didn't even feel bad about it. I was the worst friend on earth.

"I would. But I'll never cross that line unless you want me to," he said in a husky voice, and my eyes matched his.

"Jack." I abruptly moved away from him before I did something I would regret—like kiss him. I walked around the island and removed a few assorted vegetables from the fridge.

"You know, when I saw you at the event you were working at, and I watched you handle that drunk guy, I thought, *Wow, that's the kind of woman I want to get to know. Intelligent, smart, sexy ... tough as nails.* Of course, he was getting out of hand, and I wasn't going to allow him to treat you like that. I had to step in."

"You think you saved me?" I turned slightly to peer at him.

"No, I was hoping you would save me," he said, leaving me to ponder what he meant by that. "You have such a pure heart," Jack said, and I spun around, giving him my back.

"Jack, I have to work." I opened several cabinet doors before I found white ceramic bowls that I could use for tonight's occasion.

"Do you have a hard time with compliments?" He watched me from across the counter.

I was trying to control the situation of this intense chemistry between Jack and me. I hadn't signed up for this, and I was only fooling myself if I thought this wasn't going to be a problem tonight.

"I just don't appreciate being put on a pedestal. I'm nothing special. I can be really crazy," I said, knowing that would likely turn him off. *Guys didn't like crazy, right?* I opened a red bag of chips and dumped it into one of the ceramic bowls that I'd found.

"Please tell me you brought other food." He chuckled.

I glared at him. "Of course. There are several trays of appetizers in the fridge, and I have some chicken wings I can heat in the oven."

"That sounds delicious," he said, rubbing his palms together. "You sure know what poker players like to eat."

"I'm improvising a little, but I've catered my fair share of games."

He came across the island to stand very close to me. "I like your kind of crazy, by the way."

And we were back to that.

I sighed, wiping the counter. "No, you don't, Jack. I have *huge* emotional baggage. No guy likes that." I gave him a side-glance.

"I like that you're being honest," he said, and his eyes softened. "Tell me about your childhood."

"Why?"

"I want to know more about you. Am I not allowed to be curious?" Jack asked.

When he looked at me like that, how could I deny him?

I bit my lip before saying, "As a kid, I had to take care of my mom. She would never admit it, but I think she suffered from depression. Anyway, I've always had to be perfect. Get straight A's and be a good kid. I didn't want more trouble for my mother since she had my brother to take care of, and . . . well, let's just say I never really got attention, growing up. I was on my own most of the time."

"Sounds rough."

"It's a stupid thing to complain about, especially compared to what my brother had to go through," I said.

"I can tell you have a good heart, and I love that about you," Jack said.

My heart swelled just with the word *love*. I diverted my eyes to the celery sticks that I'd laid on the cutting board earlier and pulled out a knife from the drawer. Doing all this, I was aware of Jack's eyes burning on my skin.

This is going to be a long night.

"What's the matter? Did I say something wrong?" Jack inquired.

"No, well ..."

I wasn't expecting this—whatever this was between Jack and me. Today, I was supposed to come in here and help Jack host his event, and that was it, but now, being here with him made me realize that maybe I didn't despise Jack after all. In truth, I liked being around him. Only, now, there was Scarlett, and I had purposely placed her there, right between us.

I gathered my thoughts before saying, "It's just that caring too much makes you get hurt more easily, and I don't want that to happen to Scarlett." I peered at him without picturing him in bed with Scarlett. *Had they? Had they not?* At this point, I had no idea what was going on between them. I was too afraid to ask without sounding like a jealous girlfriend.

"I think I felt a chill," he said, shivering playfully. "If that look gets any icier, it could be winter in here. I thought we were having a moment, and there you go, putting Scarlett front and center." He walked around me and opened the fridge. "I wonder if she knows you're using her to hide your feelings for me," Jack said.

I was sweating. "Excuse me?" I placed the knife on the counter, the one I had been using to chop up the celery sticks.

"You heard me," he said from behind the fridge door.

"That's so insane," I fumed. "You're trying to put the focus on me because you don't want to talk about Scarlett. She has feelings for you, you know. What if she wants more from you? Can you give it to her?" I asked. "Because Scarlett thinks you feel the same about her."

"What? I don't see how that's possible." Jack closed the door without removing anything from the fridge and stood there, observing. "No, I won't be able to offer her more," he said firmly. "I won't lie about that, and I won't apologize either. If a woman falls in love with me, even when we've set boundaries, that's on her, not me."

"You are such a jerk," I growled. "Can't you see how into you she is? You took her to a charity event. That's not something you do with people you're casual about unless she's a call girl."

"I needed a date, and she was available." He shrugged. "She's fun to be around, but I could never commit myself to her . . . because she's not for me."

"You need to tell her," I demanded.

"I have. Many times."

"Tell her again," I said, picking up a corkscrew that I had placed on the counter earlier. "Because, the way she's been talking, it sounds like you guys are in a relationship," I huffed.

He flinched.

"I'm not going to stab you," I groaned. "But know that I could if you don't clear things up with Scarlett."

"How did things turn so hostile?" His eyes widened, and he took a few steps toward me. "I think your threats are empty."

"Test me and find out." I arched my brow and took a step back before realizing Jack had backed me into a corner.

"I don't know what kind of lies she's been feeding you, but I haven't seen her since that day she left my apartment. I swear," Jack said.

"I don't understand. Why would she lie?" I murmured.

"You think something happened between us?" The corners of his eyes crinkled.

"I don't care. You're both adults, and it's none of my business." I nudged past him and walked across the kitchen to open a bottle of Chianti. I should have waited until the guests arrived, but Jack was making me so nervous that I was doing everything backward.

"Victoria, nothing happened between us," he continued without missing a beat. "I took Scarlett to the event. Halfway through, she threw up all over herself. She didn't want you to know because she didn't want to disappoint you, so I brought her to my apartment to get cleaned up. Only she fell asleep on my couch. The next morning, I went to work, and when I got home, Scarlett was gone." He was now standing next to me.

Too close actually.

"I called her later and told her that I had a lovely time, but I had feelings for someone else."

"You do?" My eyes snapped up.

"You're an intelligent woman, Victoria. You know very well what's going on between us. I want you to stop pushing someone on me, thinking it's just going to make me go away. Go ahead and try your best. I'm not going anywhere." He stood there, staring.

He was right. I had been doing everything possible to make it harder for him to get close, including using Scarlett, and now, I'd made a mess of everything. I only had myself to blame. I should never have tangled myself with Jack professionally.

"I don't want to talk about it." I diverted my eyes back to the wine bottle that I was struggling with.

"No, I imagine you don't," he said in a low growl, walking away.

"Please, Jack, I have too many things to do," I said over my shoulder.

I remained in the kitchen while he went upstairs, doing who knew what. I couldn't care less. I wanted tonight to be over, now more than ever.

11

VICTORIA

SOON, the guests arrived. Eight men sat at the poker table, including Jack. There were doctors, lawyers, and a real estate agent. Some dressed casual, and those who wore suits had come to Jack's place right after work. They appeared like they were about to embark on an international business venture, and I watched them as they stuffed their faces with hors d'oeuvres and other snacks. I cut through the cloud of smoke, holding a silver tray as I served the guests, and I wondered if I would have to throw out my dress by the end of the night. I had no idea if the smell of cigar would ever come out.

Later, Jack asked me to water down the alcohol, so they would come back for more and tip better. But I didn't need to water down the drinks, as I was charming enough that they kept coming back anyway. And I thought Jack had noticed it, too, because he came around to check on me every chance he got. *Could he be jealous?* I liked to think he was.

One of the guys who hovered around me all night was a lawyer from another firm. He was a silver fox—a little too old for my liking—with a neatly trimmed beard. He leaned over the counter as far as he could to get closer. I'd bet he thought his blue eyes were enchanting enough to sway me into going out with him next Saturday, but I politely turned him down, telling him I had a boyfriend. That should put an end to things because he had no chance in hell that I would go anywhere with him.

Jeez, what is it with lawyers and me?

"Jack told me you used to volunteer at the New York Children's Hospital," he said.

I thought his name was Mark, but the men's laughter was so loud that it was difficult to hear anything at all.

"He told you that?" I asked, mixing vodka with soda.

"You don't think he did a background check before hiring you?" Mark chuckled. "He's a man of the law. I doubt he wants to get wrapped up in a scandal, no matter how beautiful that scandal is," he said, and then I smirked.

Right, Jack would do a background check. Of course, that explained how he had known about my volunteer work at the hospital.

"Thanks, I think." I looked over at Jack, who was talking up the real estate agent.

He caught my gaze, and I instantly looked away.

"Did you want to be a nurse?" Mark asked.

"Um ... well, no." I glanced up at him.

What's that look on his face?

"Do you still have that uniform?" he asked.

Ugh. I know where this is going.

"No. Candy stripers don't wear uniforms anymore." I frowned.

"That's a shame. We could have had a lot of fun with that." He winked, and my stomach churned.

Creep.

You think I would be used to getting hit on like that.

"Excuse me." I bit my tongue as I walked away.

I told myself it was better to step away than to confront him. This was Jack's night. He was fulfilling a friend's wish, raising money for the New York Children's Hospital, and that was something that was important to me, too. So, I didn't need to ruin it for him by telling one of his guests off.

I made my way to the snack table and picked up the empty silver trays when Jack strode over to my side. I was well aware of his hand resting at the small of my back.

"Everything okay?" Jack whispered in my ear.

"I think it's time for the speech," I said.

"Right." Jack nodded.

He fumbled with his phone to turn off the music, and I ended up turning it off manually. Jack thanked me with a smile. Then, he straightened his tie and turned towards the crowd of men.

"Can I have your attention, gentlemen? My friend Victoria has asked that you all listen to her while she says a few words about my charity that I've been chatting you up about all night."

"Where did you find her, Jack? She's hot!" Mark shouted from the kitchen, raising his glass.

Jack then walked over to speak to him privately. He nodded for me to continue while he took Mark's drink away. I was starting to realize why he'd wanted to water down the alcohol. When everyone turned their attention to me, I smiled, wiping my sweaty palms on my dress.

I took a deep breath before saying, "Okay ... wow. It got so quiet in here."

When my eyes found Jack's, I knew I could do this. "Um ... okay ... so, all of you are here for a very important reason. Jack wants to set up a charity for a close friend of his, and he needs your donations to kick this thing off. I don't need to beg you for your help, but I will tell you a story about why I would donate to it if I were you."

I brushed my hair from my face and continued, "A little over a year ago, I was volunteering at the New York Children's Hospital. Interacting with sick kids had always had a special place in my heart because, in my hometown, my brother was in and out of one. He had leukemia, and each time he went to the hospital, he was terrified and isolated from his friends, school, and all he cared for in his life. Luckily, we had great doctors and staff who could cheer him up with toys and a few jokes." I paused, tears welling in my eyes.

Jack looked at me, concerned, but I nodded to say that I was ready to keep going.

"Unfortunately, that hospital got shut down from lack of funding and not meeting building codes. To get back to the present, that's why the children's hospital was so important to me. When I signed up to volunteer, I met a little boy who also had leukemia. He was always cracking jokes and had much more energy than I'd thought possible for a boy in his condition. He talked to me about his godfather often and wanted us to meet. What kind of a five-year-old thinks of these things, right?" I thought of Luke's smiling face, and my knees shook.

Jack rushed to my side, turning me away from the crowd. "Are you okay?" he asked, and in the half-dark room, I thought his eyes were glistening.

"I'm fine. Let me finish," I prompted.

"Okay." Jack nodded, standing off to the side.

"Um ... that boy died last year." I glanced up at the ceiling, wiping my tears with the back of my hand. "He was such a special boy, just like my brother, Chris. They both died too young. They never got a chance to graduate from high school or get that first job. They never got the opportunity to live life." I wanted to collapse on the floor and curl into a ball, but I had some dignity remaining. "The point is that we need to do more to help find a cure for these horrible illnesses. Please donate and make a difference."

I wiped my tears and tried to laugh. Clapping my hands once, I got their attention. "Let's play some poker, shall we? Get it going, dealer."

I slapped the dealer's shoulder, and everyone continued like nothing had happened. I ran to the bathroom to pull myself together. Then, moments later, someone knocked on the door.

"Occupied!" I shouted and then splashed my cheeks with water but my eyes remained puffy. I leaned on the edge of the sink with my hands on my face. I was relieved it was finally over.

The door opened, and Jack entered. "Hey."

"Jack," I squealed, throwing a hand towel at him. "Don't you have any etiquette? I said it was occupied."

Stupid me I forgot to lock the door. Thank God I was standing over the sink instead of my butt over the toilet bowl. *Talk about dying from embarrassment.*

"I'm sorry. I just had to know that you were all right," Jack said, pushing the shower curtain away to sit on the edge of the tub across from me. "Are you okay?"

"Yeah, it just hit me harder than expected." I got up, eyeing myself in the mirror.

Oh boy. I was one hot mess.

Black mascara ran down my face. I could have passed myself off as Alice Cooper's twin. I plucked a tissue from the box on the shelf and added soap and water.

"Sorry it didn't go the way you'd wanted. I was so nervous." I gave Jack a side-glance before I removed my makeup on the right side of my face.

"No, you were great; trust me," Jack said.

"I tried to hold it together," I said, playing with the tissue, cleaning off the remaining black ink from under my eyes. "It's hard to talk about someone who means the world to you ... and then lose them."

"What was the boy's name?" His voice was tight.

When I turned, Jack was sitting there, sniffling, wiping his nose on his sleeve. It was unexpected.

"Are you crying?"

"Don't change the subject," he croaked. "We're talking about you."

"I don't want to talk anymore," I said.

With no more tissue in the blue paper box, I grabbed a fistful of toilet paper to blow my nose. Somehow seeing Jack so emotional opened the gateway of tears again.

"Is it okay if I go home? I hope I didn't ruin anything for your charity."

"No, the guys were thrilled to help me out. I'm sorry about Mark. His behavior was unacceptable." A line appeared between his brows. "I don't know why I invited him. He's just related to my partner at the firm, and for some stupid reason, I felt the urge to get in his good graces. I should have never allowed him around you."

"I've dealt with worse people." I smiled. "Is this becoming a pattern with us?"

"What is?"

"You scaring away drunk jerks for me." I shifted from the sink to face him.

"I would never let anything happen to you, Victoria." His eyes were soft, and there was something in them that made me melt. "Can I confess something to you?"

"Only if it doesn't make me cry." I flashed him a weak smile.

"It won't. I promise."

He stood and leaned against the sink next to me, arms crossed and his back to the wall, facing me. "When I saw you that night, I felt like I'd seen you before." He gestured with his outer hand.

"At another event?" I brushed my hair from my face.

"No, like in a past life ..." His mouth twitched.

I studied his face. "Oh, please," I said, settling down on the long bench by the sink because this close to Jack was causing friction inside of me.

"Hear me out," he said, crouching beside me. "Isn't it possible that we could be connected by our souls? We could have been horses galloping through the grassy plains together, for all I know. Don't you feel it? You've come back to me, and I always knew you would."

I raised my eyebrows and burst out laughing. I couldn't stop laughing until someone knocked on the door to use the bathroom.

"It's occupied," Jack yelled out.

"You know you're not funny, right?" I stared at him.

"Said the girl who's laughing."

Just then, Jack stood and chuckled. "But I got you to laugh, so that's what's important," he said, holding a hand out. "You should have seen the look on your face. It was priceless!"

"Thanks for that, Jack. I really needed a laugh." I slapped his back, and we exited the room. "You sure had me going there for a second," I said sarcastically.

"You're not crying anymore; that's all I care about. I hate to see you like that."

He brushed my cheek before hugging me in the little hallway that led to the main living area. For a moment, I forgot what I had been crying about in the first place. It felt nice, safe, to be surrounded by his arms.

I pulled away and smoothed out my dress. "I think I should go home, if that's okay."

"I'll drive you." Jack peered down at me.

"No, you need to stay here."

"I can wrap things up," he said quickly. "Why don't you wait here, and I'll send everyone home? You've already refused my driver once, and you're in no condition to travel in a cab to get home."

"I don't want to ruin your night," I said. "I'll be fine in a cab."

"Always thinking of others." He shook his head. "Let me drive you. I'll even take you out for a bite as a thank-you for allowing me the pleasure."

"You want to reward me for allowing you to take me home? Wow, a girl doesn't have to do much for you to spoil her." I rubbed my eyes and yawned.

"I just don't want this night to end with you." He bit his bottom lip before saying, "I need to talk to you about something."

Talk? Maybe to tally up the cost for tonight's food and decorations?

"I don't know ..." My stomach rumbled, and Jack met my eyes. "Well, maybe I'm a little hungry. I'll consider it if you're in the mood for something simple." I had been so busy with preparing for tonight's event that I didn't have time to eat anything all day.

"Simple is the only thing I know." One side of his lips went up. "I'll tell you what. I'll treat you to a burger."

"Do you know what the inside of a burger joint looks like, Mr. Hotshot?"

"Better than you." He winked.

There was nothing simple about Jack Turner, or maybe that was what I'd made him out to be in my head.

"Maybe it's better I go home. Thanks for the offer, but I'm kind of tired. I'll take a cab home."

"You are extremely stubborn. Do you really want to start an argument with a lawyer? I guarantee that you will lose. I can stand here all night, debating with you, and then you might as well stay over. What's it going to be? My house or yours?"

"Jack are you coming?" Jack's attention goes back to the rowdy men sitting at the poker table.

"You should stay here with your friends."

"Those are acquaintances, not friends," Jack said, his eyes

leaving the group of men to find mine. "I do have an opening for one if you're interested."

"Is that what we're defined as? We'll be back to me blatantly rejecting you while you beg for my attention." I smiled slyly.

"You think highly of yourself, don't you?" He chuckled.

"You so easily fuel the fire. I can tell I'm the one thing you want that you can't have for a fling."

"What makes you think that's what I'm looking for?" His eyes met mine, and I saw something in them that made me think I had been wrong.

"Isn't that what you do?"

He smirked. "Just wait here."

Jack left to round up his guests and escort them out. I waited, leaning against the wall with my arms crossed. I knew I shouldn't go anywhere with Jack because the tension between us just kept building up. And, when I thought I had him all figured out, another layer was peeled back, revealing something I never imagined about him—that he could be sensitive and fun to be around.

When Jack returned, he held out his arm for me to hold. "Shall we?"

I stared at him and then walked to the door, ignoring his chivalry.

"Sure, play hard to get." He chuckled.

I paused and circled back around, slipping my hand around his bicep.

"Look at that. You're finally warming up to me," he teased.

"Don't push it."

We walked in silence to the elevator and then a block from his building to reach the parking garage he owned to store all of his cars. The indoor parking lot was surprisingly well lit with security guarding the merchandise twenty-four/seven. I walked down a row with a Lexus, Ferrari, Porsche, and a Rolls-Royce and then another row with the same cars but different colors.

"Is this a luxury car dealership? I mean, really, how many do you need?" I asked breathlessly. I stopped in front of a Porsche and admired its shine, like it hadn't been used since it was driven into the underground parking lot. "You're only one guy, and I bet you don't even drive half of them."

"These aren't all mine," he said, standing tall beside me, proud to show off his babies. "Some of my friends pay me to store their cars for them. I've got another garage on the east side, but those ones are mine," he said, pulling the keys to the Porsche out of his pocket and walking to the passenger's side. "I'm hungry. Ready to go?"

"Still hungry after all that food from tonight?" I asked, sliding through the open door that Jack held opened for me.

"I'm a big boy. No offense but finger food is not going to cut it."

I nodded and settled into the seat, quickly putting on my seat belt.

"Do you want to drive?" He gave me a side look.

"You're not going to let me do that." I peered over him.

He smiled. "You're right; I'm only teasing. This one is my baby, and I need to know you at least a year before I allow you anywhere near my stick."

He winked, revved the engine, and tore out of the parking garage, barely waiting for the gate leading out to the street to open. I clutched the edge of my seat as he ripped down the road. It wasn't that he was a terrible driver. He was actually skilled at weaving through New York traffic. Each motion was fluid, like he'd done this a million times before. He probably did, constantly showing off to his dates, but I wasn't a date ... not even his friend.

12

JACK

SOON, we reached my favorite burger joint, which was open until midnight. We sat in a booth in the corner, and Victoria ordered the meatiest burger on the menu along with a side of onion rings and a milkshake. It was refreshing to see that Victoria didn't care what I thought. I would always meet these women who counted calories or were afraid to eat in front of me. I guessed they thought that I might judge them.

But I love a hungry woman.

That was one of the reasons I found Victoria so interesting. She never felt the need to impress me or pretend to be something she was not, and I found that very attractive in a woman.

"You didn't eat today?" I observed carefully.

Her eyes darted around the room. "Um . . . well, no. I never do while I'm working. I try to eat well, but sometimes, I don't have time, or I'm just too lazy to cook something for myself."

She gathered her hair up and wrapped the elastic twice around her bun. Strands of hair trickled around her face, and I smiled. Victoria was beautiful without any makeup, though she never wore too much. She didn't need to.

Simply naturally stunning.

"You need someone to take care of yourself better." I placed the set of utensils aside and leaned in on my elbows.

"I take care of myself just fine," she said, fiddling with her glass of water.

"I didn't mean that in a negative way," I said. "I just meant that you take care of everybody else. Don't you want someone to take care of you?"

Before she could say anything, the waitress came with our food. I quickly dug in while admiring the mom-and-pop-style diner with the checkered floors. The pungent smell of grease flowed through my nostrils, and I felt like I was back in my element. It was always nice to wind down in a down-to-earth place after being surrounded by the elites of New York.

"I have Scarlett, and she takes care of me," she said after a short moment.

"She's way needier than you'll ever be. Sorry, but I like to call it the way I see it." I shrugged.

"Why do you keep talking like you know me?" Victoria placed her burger down and picked up a napkin instead.

"Because I see you, and it's like looking at myself before I became this." I gestured to my physique.

She giggled. "What? The successful and powerful attorney?"

"No." I snorted. "A man who's been taken advantage of too many times for his generosity. It can only make you fold into yourself." I picked up my burger and took a bite.

"But I'm not bitter," she pointed out.

Does she think I am?

"No, but it's only a matter of time before you will be. I know what it's like to go above and beyond to do things for other people and then get the short end of the stick."

"Are you talking about a woman?" She tilted her head to the side.

"You're making fun of my situation again?" I grinned. "Can you get your mind off of my stick and—"

"No. I didn't mean because you said sti—um ... whatever." She rubbed her temple, and her cheeks flushed. "I meant ... it sounds like a woman made you build this wall around you."

How could she possibly know? Am I that transparent?

Victoria made me want to lay everything out for her. My past, my feelings for her ... but I couldn't, not yet. Not when her father was one of my clients. No, I would have to refrain from getting involved with Victoria. At least until I figured out what was the best thing to do.

"I plead the fifth," I said, shifting in my seat. "Anyhow, we're talking about you."

Her eyes dragged over my face before looking back down at her plate. "Maybe you're right. I do too many things for people like Scarlett. I know she doesn't appreciate it."

"Of course I'm right. You should agree with me often. That way, we would both be right." I flashed her a smile.

"Cute. I didn't know lawyers were so funny." She rolled the napkin between her hands and dropped it next to her plate. Then, she reached over and stole a fry from my dish.

"I'm a lot of things, if you give yourself the chance to get to know me," I said with a mouthful.

"All right, so tell me more about yourself." She licked the salt off her fingers, and my eyes couldn't help but be drawn to her mouth.

Full, luscious lips. I wonder how they taste.

"Well, I grew up with parents who struggled to make ends meet, so I understand the full value of hard work and dedication. I have never once taken a bribe or had money that I hadn't earned. I am an honest man, believe it or not."

"Just not in the courtroom. You defend bad guys." Victoria took a bite of her burger.

"I defend who pays me. It's my job."

"You can choose what cases you take. You're a partner," she said.

"And I'm good at corporate law. These guys have been my clients for years, and I wouldn't dream of turning my back on them or tarnishing my own reputation."

"What's your goal, Jack?" Her eyes trailed over my face.

"My goal is to finish this burger." I took another huge bite and then wiped my mouth with the napkin.

"I mean, a long-term goal. Are you going to run in the same circles until you retire?" She studied me closely.

"Why shouldn't I? I've got a good thing going. I'm the youngest partner in my firm—which is all any lawyer ever wants—and my name is on the building, no less. I can have any woman I want—well, almost any woman—and money is no obstacle for me. Guys would kill for this life because it's a great one."

"But are you happy?" she asked.

My heart compressed. Leave it to Victoria to be such a killjoy, but she was right. Only I was not sure how far to let her in. What would she think if she had a look on the inside? What if she knew the truth about me?

"There's more to life than being happy, Victoria." I straightened my shoulders.

"I can take a hint. You're obviously not." She raises her eyebrows at me.

"What was the kid's name?" I asked.

After tonight, I was pretty sure I knew who he was. All I needed was for her to confirm my suspicions.

She groaned. "Again with the question for an answer."

"Was it Luke?" I said.

Her eyes slowly met mine. Every bone in my body ached ... and my heart broke through my rib cage every time I uttered his name.

"How did you know that?" she said in a half-whisper.

"I was his godfather," I said, knowing I would have to tell her more, but this was as far as I could bring myself to say.

She reached across the table and hesitantly placed one hand on top of mine. "Luke? Luke Taylor was your godson?"

I nodded and hoped she ignored the dampness in my eyes that I was trying to hold back with all of my might, and I was grateful she'd averted her gaze to stare at our unmoving hands.

My hand was slowly warming from her touch, and neither of us said a word. We didn't finish our food, and it got cold by the time she broke the silence.

"Should you call a driver to bring you home?" she asked. "I can make it the rest of the way on my own."

Silence remained until I cleared my throat. "I'll drive you like I promised. Do you need to stop anywhere on the way?"

Victoria shook her head, neither of us looking at each other.

I stood and opened the door for her as we walked out.

A few minutes after we were on the road again, I said, "I didn't mean to put a damper on your evening. It's just ... the way Luke spoke about you, I felt like I knew you. Who would have thought, one day, you'd be right here next to me?"

"It's nice to finally meet you, Jay." Her voice was strained.

"You, too, Vicky."

There was a moment of silence that passed between us before Victoria said, "So, you figured it all out when I gave the speech earlier?"

"To be honest, I thought I'd seen you around at the hospital, but when you mentioned a boy battling leukemia and his godfather, I put two and two together."

"Funny he wanted to match us up," she said, looking out the passenger window. "Maybe he saw something in us that we don't."

"Luke was a special boy. Sometimes, I thought he was maturer than I was. When he died ... it broke me."

"I know. It devastated me, too." She looked down at her hands.

As I watched her sitting there, something came over me. It had felt so foreign that I couldn't remember the last time I'd felt this way.

"All my life, I had been looking for meaning, and I knew, if I worked hard enough, I would achieve it. When my career took off and it brought me money, I thought, *I made it*. And it should have made me happy, but it wasn't until Luke was born that I realized everything else seemed so petty ... so senseless," I said, feeling her eyes on me. "Luke was the light of my life, and even though I wasn't able to spend every minute with him, he was always on my mind. Then, when I lost him . . . it was as though the light went out. Until . . . "

"Until what?" She looked up with those alluring eyes.

I had known, when Victoria came into my life, it was like I'd found new meaning, but how would I begin to tell her? I was a man who didn't do well when it came to expressing his emotions.

I needed her in my life. She was good for me. Even a little boy had known that.

When it came to love, I didn't know my way around. It was like walking in the dark, but with Victoria, I was willing to find my way, to go the distance. The words were stuck in my throat.

I love her.

My heart stopped at the realization, and I swerved to the side of the road and slammed on the brakes. When I did, she snapped up her chin, locking our gazes. I had no willpower left. She had managed to take everything out of me, and when she sat there, giving me a questioning look, I answered it the only way I knew how. My hand went behind her head and guided her lips to mine.

She responded with equal eagerness, tugging at the collar of my jacket, pulling me closer.

"You are so beautiful. You bring in the light, Victoria," I told her. "You asked me if I was happy," I added, biting my lip. "I am when I'm around you."

"Jack," she sighed heavily. "I don't want you to say those things to me," she whispered.

"Why not?" I pulled back to look at her.

"Because I can't be with you. Scarlett has feelings for you."

"Victoria, she doesn't even know me." I chuckled.

"I know, but—"

"I have no interest in Scarlett. If I did, I wouldn't be here with you." I brushed the hair away from her face.

"But Scarlett is my friend and ..."

"And, if she was your friend, she would be happy for you."

She diverted her gaze from me to the front window. "I can't. I just can't hurt her like that, no matter what I feel for you." Her eyes found mine again.

"What is it you want, Victoria?"

"I want you to drive me home, please," she said, her voice strained.

13

VICTORIA

I REMAINED FROZEN IN PLACE, leaning against the back of my door. My heart pounded, and it felt like the kiss with Jack was an out-of-body experience. Slowly, I started piecing together what had just happened. But how could I allow myself to get this far with Jack, allow myself to fall for him?

My stomach churned with uneasiness when I heard something coming from Scarlett's room. Then, I realized what it was. Scarlett's wailing cries. I didn't even think as I lunged inside to see her surrounded by used tissues and chocolate wrappers. *Had she found my stash?*

This only meant one thing—Jack Turner.

I rushed to sit beside her body, which was sprawled along the length of the bed. I moved the hair stuck to her tear-stained cheeks and dabbed her runny nose with the last tissue in the box she held.

"What's wrong, Scar? Talk to me." I placed my black-and-gold clutch purse on her nightstand.

She exploded into another wailing sob, trying to speak. I couldn't understand a word.

"What can I get you? Water, wine?" I asked.

"I don't need more wine," she said, sounding congested. "That won't fix my broken heart. I found the good stuff you hid in the bathroom cupboard."

"I was saving that for a special occasion," I said, trying to be funny or to hide the guilt off my face.

I'd kissed Jack Turner, and I'd liked it. I was a horrible, horrible friend.

"They're stale," she groaned, pointing to the half-empty box of chocolate.

"And you ate them anyway?" This was bad, and it was all my fault. "Sit up," I said, pushing against her dead weight as I squeezed my way onto the bed. I swatted away tissues as her head fell into my lap. I started stroking her hair. "Is it Jack?" I gulped.

"Don't even say his name!" she squealed, and her high pitch made my hair stand on end.

"What did Jack do?"

Questions swirled through my mind, wondering if he'd told her about the kiss. No, he wouldn't. There wouldn't have been time for him to call her when he dropped me off and me to make it up to our apartment. With the amount of tissues and the alcohol consumed, it couldn't have happened that quickly.

"Scar, talk to me. What did he do?"

"He called me," she whimpered. "Before his poker night started ... he called and told me that I should stop calling him and leaving him messages. That he's sorry that he didn't make it clear enough that there's nothing between us."

She wailed again, and I rocked her head. Jack must have sneaked away to call her after we talked in the kitchen when I told him to make things clear with Scarlett. But I hadn't thought he was going to do this tonight.

"Shh, shh, it's okay," I said nervously.

I knew she would be angry with me once she found out the

truth, but then again, I should be upset. *Why had she lied, making me believe that they were an item when they weren't? Wait ... had she sent herself those roses last week?* I guessed it wasn't a good time to confront her with it.

I cleared my throat. "Did he say why?"

"Why? Why do you think? He's a player ..." She was using my words. The truth was more complicated than that. "I'm never dating another man again. I would date women if they weren't so dramatic."

"You're just angry right now," I said softly, helping her sit up straight.

I went to get another tissue box, and when I came back, she was already cleaning up her mess.

"You were right, Vicky," she said, angrily smashing tissues into the garbage can. "I was in too deep before I really got a chance to know him. I'm such an idiot! You warned me so many times, and it was over before it even started. Why do I always do this?" She collapsed and buried her head into her pillow.

I hesitantly walked to her and rubbed her back. "You can't blame yourself, Scarlett. You need to find someone who appreciates you for you," I said, knowing they'd only technically known each other for a day. I didn't get it; how could she have fallen for someone so quickly?

Again, not a good time to ask.

"You're the smart one, Vicky," she said, shaking her head. "You're picky about who you go out with because it keeps you safe. You know not to jump into any relationship without careful consideration. Why can't I do that? Why can't I be the smart one who knows how to look after herself? I'm so stupid."

"Stop blaming yourself. I might have had something to do with it when I threatened him and said I knew he would hurt you." I braced myself for the backlash, tightly shutting my eyes.

She sniffled, sitting up. "What?" Leaning back, she settled

into a cross-legged position. "You're the reason he dumped me?" she asked calmly.

Is she serious? They weren't even dating.

I looked at her and swallowed hard before saying, "There's no way to know if I'm the actual reason, but I did make a big case against you two being together," I said, and she gasped. "Hear me out. He told me he didn't see anything happening between you two. I knew you liked him a lot, so I thought it was best to intervene—"

"Oh. My. *God*! Do you ever know how to mind your own business?" She stood and wiped her nose on the sleeves of her pajama shirt, straightened her sweatpants, and pulled her hair into a ponytail. "I might look like I'm losing my mind, but I'm still a grown adult. This is just like the time in college when you tried to break me and Dylan up."

"He was cheating on you!" I scoffed.

"And that was my information to know, not yours. You had no right to get involved, yet you still did. It's like you think I don't know how to take care of myself, like I'm this baby who needs your help all the time."

"I don't think that." I glanced up at her.

"You act like it!" She threw her hands in the air and rubbed her temples. "You couldn't help yourself. You're the one who scared him off," she said.

I crossed my arms and looked at her like an authoritative parent. "I didn't scare him off. It's not my fault he's not interested in you."

She gasped. "There's your judgmental look again. You're just jealous that Jack was paying me all the attention that night at the bar. Are you trying to steal him away from me?"

"You know I would never do that," I said, flipping my hair from my eyes.

If Jack and Scarlett had been an item, I would have never

interfered. I would have never kissed him. But, when Jack had told me that there was nothing between them ... well, that made him a free agent and Scarlett a liar.

"That's right," she said in an overly kind voice. "Because Princess Victoria Fairfax, Duchess of Angel Town, never does anything wrong." She folded her hands and rested them against her cheeks while batting her eyelashes. "Can you see the halo?" She drew a circle over my head and then danced around me while singing a cheery song.

I stood up. "You're being immature."

"That's how you see me anyway, so why not live up to the standards?"

"This is childish. Can we talk like adults?" I held out my arms.

"I don't want to talk to you. In fact, I don't ever want to see your face again. I'm giving you a month."

"A month for what?" I replied.

"To move out. My name is on the lease, so I have full control. Move."

My face turned pale. "You can't kick me out over one little argument."

"Little?" She laughed. "Of course this is little to you. I thought I'd finally found someone I could get serious about, and you ruined it for me."

"Oh my God! It was *one* date! And he took you out because I asked him to!" I paused. "Anyhow, you've been lying to me all along, making me believe what you had with Jack was something more," I said, walking toward the door. "You haven't seen each other since the charity event."

She turned pale. "How do you know that?"

"Because he told me," I said, and the color on her face went paler than the white sheets on her bed. "What did you think,

Scarlett, that I wasn't going to find out?" I walked back to grab my purse from her nightstand. "You can keep the apartment ..."

Oh, and Jack is a good kisser, by the way! I wanted to say, but I didn't.

I swung the door behind me shut and walked to my room. *Was I living in some alternate universe where my hatred had transferred from Jack to Scarlett?* I shrank to the floor and contemplated how this entire day had panned out. And, the way Scarlett had been behaving tonight, I was not even sure if it was a relationship worth fixing. Either way, I needed to get some sleep.

14

VICTORIA

I'D THOUGHT rest would help, but I was more hurt and confused than ever when I got out of bed the next morning. I called Scarlett's name, but she didn't answer. Her bedroom door was open, and her breakfast dishes sat on the counter. She had left me a note that said she would be gone all day with an obscene drawing at the bottom. I'd thought her anger last night was the alcohol talking, but I guessed she hated me that much.

After breakfast, I didn't know what to do with myself. I needed a plan to make things right, but I wasn't sure who to start with—Scarlett or Jack.

My entire life was usually wrapped around work. Scarlett and I normally worked at my second job together, and we hadn't ever had any issues—until now. It was going to be awkward, working together tomorrow night. I would give her time to cool off, but deep down, I knew our relationship would never be the same.

Just before lunch, I texted Jack, but when he didn't respond, I decided to go to his house. I felt that there was still unfinished business between us, and there was more I should have told him.

The kiss had taken me by surprise. I hadn't had time to process what I was feeling or even knew how he really felt about me. Maybe it was an accumulation of our emotions.

As I got into a cab, I listened to the music on my phone to distract myself from yesterday's thoughts. I felt like, last night, I'd had a connection with Jack, but I had to make sure it wasn't only because of Luke ... of the loss we both shared.

By the time I reached Jack's apartment building, my stomach grumbled loudly. I should have eaten before, but I was determined to come here. Walking up to the reception desk, I waited for Sam to finish with his phone call.

He smiled at me and mouthed that he wouldn't be long. When he hung up, he asked, "Is Mr. Turner expecting you?"

"No, not exactly," I said nervously. "Is he in today?"

"I saw him leave early this morning," he replied, studying me from under the visor of his hat. "I know where he goes every Saturday, but I'm not sure if you're supposed to know that."

"Please, Sam. We had a good chat when I came yesterday. Aren't we friends?" I gave him a sweet smile. "I really need to see Jack. It's crucial. Where is he?"

He fiddled with the pockets of his coat. "Mr. Turner is a private man, and I don't think it's a good idea to share that information with anyone."

"I understand ..." I trailed off.

"What is this about?" He cast me a curious look. "I mean, it's none of my business, but if it's a matter of love or death, I might feel obliged to give out the information."

"Oh, no. Jack and I are not ... together." I laughed nervously.

He smiled, pleased with my answer. "You must be someone special. It's been a long time since he brought a woman into his apartment or trusted one to go in there herself."

"He doesn't?"

That's odd.

But then again, I had been there for business.

"He's at church," Sam said finally.

"Church?"

"Yes, with a cemetery behind it." He ripped a scrap piece of paper from a notebook. "I won't tell you which one, and I won't write it on this paper for you to read when it flies off the desk. Got it?"

"Subtle." I smiled as he slid the paper in my direction. It stopped at my feet, and I picked it up to see the chicken-scratch writing that read *Stevenson Lake Cemetery*.

I didn't know where that was, so I called a cab to take me there.

LATER, once I reached the parking lot by the church, I leaned through the partition and asked, "If I give you extra, would you mind waiting here for me?" I wasn't sure if I would find Jack or if he wanted to see me right now. "I promise I won't be long."

"I can't wait around for one person. Do you know how many people need to get around in this city?"

"I guess that's a no," I said, paying him.

He looked at me dead in the eye and said, "Get out of my cab, or I'll charge you double."

"Okay, okay," I said, sliding out the door.

He sped off before I could shut the door properly. I was starting to see a pattern. I seemed to be making everyone upset these days.

I stared at the church before I walked along the dewy grass, down the rows of tombstones and the occasional flowers. I must have circled the cemetery three times before I finally found Jack.

I saw him in the distance with a bouquet of flowers. Suddenly, I felt like maybe I shouldn't be here and wanted to hide behind a tree, but there was none in sight. Slowly, I walked up to the tombstone, and Jack didn't notice me as his head was bowed. When I reached his side, I grabbed his shoulder, and he flinched.

"Victoria?" he said, shaking his head. "What are you doing here? How did you know where to find me?"

"I'm friendlier with Sam than you are." I smiled shyly, not sure if he was happy to see me. "Look, I didn't like the way things had ended between us last night ... so I needed to see you," I said in a half-whisper. I looked down at the grave and realized why he was here. My heart swelled with pain. "Oh ... *Luke.*" My throat tightened. "I have never been here before. I wanted to come to the funeral, but the attendance was limited to those invited," I said.

"Luke's mother wanted it that way." Jack's eyes brushed the sky before meeting my eyes.

He heaved a giant sigh before diverting his eyes back to the grave. "I wasn't in the country the day Luke died, and I'm totally gutted," he said all of a sudden. "I'll never forgive myself."

"The way he spoke about you, I know Luke loved you. He wouldn't want you to be so hard on yourself." I placed my hand on his shoulder.

"How can you be so sure? You didn't know him like I did. You don't know what his favorite color was, how fat he was when he was born, or when he missed his first day of school because he was sick and cried for hours. You don't know any of that, and yet you formed a stronger bond with him than I did."

"That's not true. Why would you say that?" I knelt and arranged the flowers in the bouquet wrapped in plastic to look more appealing.

"You must have spent every day with him. From the way he talked about you, it was like you were his best friend. His eyes glowed when he ranted and raved about the way you read books with different voices and the extra Jell-O you brought to him. You were his favorite person in the world, and that was why he wanted me to meet you."

"Jack, I was just doing my job," I said softly, picking at the grass, not ready to look him in the eye. "I was just a temporary replacement when his real family wasn't there. That could never diminish the bond you had with him. He knew that you loved him, so you don't have to be insecure about that." I stood, but he still wouldn't face me. My heart pounded as I awaited an explosion inside me.

"It's more complicated than that," Jack said.

"So, explain it to me."

"I just wanted . " He turned away from me, making it more frustrating that he wasn't allowing me in.

"What?"

"Forget it," he huffed. "I don't understand why I'm telling you all of this. We knew the same little boy. What does that make us?" he asked.

I felt the pain in his eyes and the hurt in my heart. I knew he was just as confused as I was. We had been brought together for reasons we didn't understand—until now. We were stuck, not able to move on from the loss. Maybe we could help each other heal and proceed with our lives. I knew that was what Luke would have wanted, but staring at Jack, I knew it wouldn't be easy.

"You're angry because I was his friend? I loved him, too, you know."

"I'm not angry about that." He lifted his gaze to meet mine. "I'm glad he found someone like you in his life, caring about him and making his stay at the hospital as comfortable as possible."

"What is it you're not telling me, Jack?" I stepped closer to him.

"I've been holding on to a secret for the longest time, and it's killing me ..." He rubbed his eyes with his thumb and index finger.

I wanted to know, but I didn't want to force it out. I wanted him to tell me because he trusted me.

"I want to show you something," he finally said.

"Right now?"

"Yes, I want to show you Luke's favorite place."

I peered into his loving eyes and grabbed his hand. "Lead the way."

WE WALKED BACK to his car in the church parking lot, and then he drove us to a two-story bookstore with a learning center for kids with disabilities. Inside, the shelves were stacked all the way to the ceiling, and children were running around like the store was a playground.

"This place is the reason Luke loved reading so much," Jack said, allowing his eyes to take in the room. "It's the reason I keep donating to this organization."

He slid my hand into his, and we slowly moved away from the entrance, weaving through rows of books and dodging excited children.

Looking up, I saw the massive mural on the ceiling, which was just an optical illusion of the sky. "That's cool," I said, pointing up.

"Luke thought that it was a portal to a fictional world," Jack explained as we climbed the staircase. "He said that, if I closed my eyes and imagined my favorite place while standing under it, it would suck me up and take me there."

"Sounds like Luke." I grinned, following Jack to the back corner of the store.

There was a kid-sized play cottage with books strewed on the floor. It had a red roof and plastic flowers around the edges.

Jack opened the door and gestured for me to go inside. "After you."

"Are you kidding? I can't fit in there." I laughed.

"What are you talking about? There's tons of room." He bent down, disappearing through the small door. "Come on. Where is your inner child?" Jack said from inside the house. When I glared at him through the tiny window, he could only shoot me a grin. "You're no fun, Victoria."

I couldn't believe he was going to make me do this. I glanced around before getting on my hands and knees, crawling inside, pushing my back against the side wall.

What a combination. Jack and close spaces were too close for comfort.

"Nice and cozy." I was aware our knees touched. "Why are we in here? Are we looking at real estate?" I said.

Jack smiled like he was enjoying this. "I brought you here because, every time I have something to tell you, you make me chase you around." He allowed his eyes to drag across my face and only stop when they reached my lips. "The way I see it, you have nowhere to go."

"What did you want to tell me?" I asked, feeling the heat from Jack's body.

Every time I was around Jack, there was always this chemistry between us that seemed to sizzle, and just when I thought he might kiss me, he pulled back and pointed at the ceiling where there was a sticker of a giraffe peeling at the edges.

"Luke loves giraffes."

"He did." I smiled.

"God, I miss him." He paused, clearing his throat. "Under the sticker, Luke wrote his name in marker. I didn't want him to get in trouble, so I paid a kid ten bucks to give me one of his stickers."

"Only you would buy off a kid." I gave him a side-glance.

"I was protecting my family."

"From a store clerk?" I smiled and ran my finger along the giraffe's neck.

"He got so mad when I covered up his name."

"He threw a fit? That's not like him." I frowned.

Jack opened one of the windows and then pretended to warm his hands on the fireplace sticker beside us, and I laughed.

"Luke told me that dogs mark their territory." Jack smiled. "Yeah, so he took to writing his name on everything as the same gesture." He chuckled. "He said he wanted this to be his house forever."

"He had a good home though, didn't he?" I asked.

"Of course, but he had this idea that he would be moving into the hospital as his permanent home when he was diagnosed. He loved this little house, and he used to spend hours in here."

"How did you explain that to him?"

Jack shrugged. "I probably told him something about how the hospital wouldn't last forever, and he'd be back in his own bed soon. I sure made myself into a big, fat liar, didn't I?"

I placed my hand on his knee and looked into his eyes. "You couldn't have known what would happen to him."

"No. No one did." He leaned forward.

I said, "What are we doing here, Jack?" I looked up at him, and suddenly, it didn't feel claustrophobic anymore.

"I want to be with you, Victoria." His voice was low and husky. "What do I have to do to convince you?"

"You ... *what*?" I bumped my head on the ceiling as I tried to get up. I felt the heat running through me, and my brain pounded, trying to comprehend what I was hearing.

His hand instinctively went to where I'd hit my head. "Are you okay?" he said, concern in his eyes.

"Yes." *No.* "You want to be with me?" I asked, knowing very well I was worth his time, but I wanted him to give me a good reason he wanted me in his life.

"Why don't we give it a shot? It's something Luke would have wanted. It's what I want ... unless you don't."

"What if we are making it out more than it is?"

"Why don't we start with this? I have somewhere to be tonight, and I was wondering if you would like to come along."

My heart lurched to a stop. "Are you asking me out or using me as a prop? I'm not interested in being just another woman hanging on your arm for the world to see."

He turned on his shoulder to face me. "You could never be a prop, Victoria. Never. You outshine any woman." His eyes burned with heat. "I'll pick you up tonight at seven."

15

VICTORIA

WHEN I ARRIVED at my apartment, Scarlett was watching some romantic comedy on TV with a bowl of popcorn resting in her lap.

"I thought you'd be out all day," I said, making my way to the couch.

She let me sit beside her, and I waited for any reaction. As of this morning, we still weren't on talking terms.

Calmly, she placed the bowl on the table and turned to me.

Her face was serious, and with hurt hiding behind her eyes, she said, "I'm sorry I overreacted. It's just that I always get the guy, and it was obvious that Jack was into you and not me. I didn't know what to do. I lashed out, and that was *so* not cool of me. Do you think you could ever forgive me?"

"Of course I forgive you. I'm the one that meddled in the first place."

Scarlett held my hands and soberly peered at me. "Tell me the truth, and I promise I won't get mad."

"The truth about what?" I gave her a once-over.

"Do you have feelings for Jack?"

My heart skipped a beat. "Um ... what? No," I replied.

Coward.

"You were never a good liar." She snorted.

I looked at her for the longest moment and said, "I don't know, Scarlett." I bit my lip. "I don't know if we have this connection because of Luke or if there's something more between us," I said.

She scrunched her brows. "Luke?"

"Remember I told you once that Luke wanted to set me up with his godfather?"

"Yeah."

"It just so happens that it's Jack."

"Seriously?" Her eyes widened.

"Anyway, that's not important. I'm sorry, Scar. I never meant for this to happen."

"It's not your fault. You can't help who you love, right?" She shrugged.

When I didn't feel the need to correct her about the *love* part, it made it clear to me that my feelings for Jack ran deep. The only thing was, part of me still viewed Jack as one of those rotten lawyers he partnered himself with even though he had proven time and time again that he was different.

"Anyhow, it wouldn't have worked out. Jack is too high maintenance for me. I need someone who revolves around me, not the other way around." She shrugged. Then, she got up and went into the kitchen.

I got up and followed her, knowing this conversation was far from being over.

Scarlett closed the fridge, and I turned, leaning against it.

"He likes you. You should be happy about that," she said, wounded. "I know I wasn't the greatest person to be around yesterday, but I was super emotional. I said a lot of crappy things, but I didn't really mean them. All of them anyway. I'm trying to do better. I really am. I don't want to be that immature brat that I was yesterday. I've never wanted to be that person, but it's so easy to when you're around to take care of me. I guess I've become pretty dependent on you, huh?"

"I'm part of the blame. I should have been honest with you and myself ... that I had feelings for Jack." I swallowed.

"I wouldn't mind if you guys started seeing each other," she said.

I looked up to see her eyes glowing with a mixture of happiness and regret. I flashbacked to the time we'd met in elementary school, and she'd tried to get to the swing set before me. "I guess I was jealous of you."

"Me? Why would you be jealous?" I blinked.

"Because I knew all along that a guy like Jack would be interested in you because of your name. You're a Fairfax. How can I compete with that?"

"I can't believe you said that." I pushed off the fridge. "You're being ridiculous."

"Where are you going?"

"Out," I said firmly. I wanted to say with Jack, but remembering our childhood together, I couldn't hurt her again and felt awkward telling her. Jack and I would be seeing more of each other, so she might as well get used to it. But I didn't want to get into all that tonight.

I walked to my bedroom, and after scouring my entire wardrobe, I decided to wear an ankle-length blue dress with cap sleeves that I had worn to a wedding last summer and paired it with a silver necklace.

When I was ready to go, I put on a long coat and wrapped my black purse over my shoulder. A text came from Jack, who was waiting downstairs.

"I'm not sure when I'll be back, but I'll text you updates," I said.

"Don't worry about me," Scarlett said coolly. "Have fun."

Even though she pretended to be okay with it, I could still feel resentment toward me.

———

HEADING DOWNSTAIRS, I saw an unexpected sight, and I smiled. I'd thought I would see a town car with a hired driver on the sidewalk. Instead, I saw Jack leaning against a sports car. He was dressed in a tuxedo, similar to the one he had worn when we first met.

"Wow, you take my breath away." Jack said.

His eyes gleamed, and my heart did a somersault.

"What is this?" I asked, slowly stepping forward. "I thought you were sending a car for me."

"I couldn't wait to see you, so I came to get you myself," he said, handing me a rose.

"I didn't know Jack Turner did romantic, cheesy stuff." I giggled, inhaling its sweet scent.

"I do." He chuckled. "I'm trying to woo you." His voice was low and husky, and it sent shivers down my back.

"Just be yourself. That's all I need," I said, meeting his gaze before he helped me into his car. I sat back, listening to soft music playing in the background. "What kind of benefit is this?" I asked, completely in the dark as to where we were going.

"It's for promoting literacy and raising money for school supplies in third-world countries," Jack said, pressing a button and starting the ignition of his car. "It's taking place at my friend's house, and he's very formal. If anything is out of place, like an untucked shirt or a missing earring, he'll throw you out for sure."

I gasped and grabbed my earring-less earlobe. "Jeez, what kind of friends do you have?" I frowned.

"I was kidding." Jack chuckled. "You nervous?" With his eyes never leaving the road, he grabbed my hand and pulled it toward him, kissing the inner part of my wrist.

"I'm a little nervous about going to this," I confirmed.

"I can tell, but why?" he asked, raising his eyes to mine.

"I've never gone to one of these upscale events unless I was working with the catering firm. I don't know how to talk to these people without thinking they see me as lesser than them."

"Victoria, they definitely will not see you as less," he said.

Was he saying that because of my name? And this was the first time I realized that I might not be able to fit into his world.

"You feel like you don't fit in because you don't."

I peered at him in disbelief. "Way to sugarcoat it. So, I don't belong? Then, why are you bringing me?" I asked, fidgeting with my sleeves.

"You'll never fit in because you are better than they are. You're not superficial, and you don't need to impress anyone. You're authentic, and that's what I love about you."

He placed his hand over mine, and I almost rested my head on his shoulder, but I stopped myself.

"Besides, the only place you belong is with me." Jack shot me a grin. "Going to these parties was becoming increasingly lonely, and with you by my side, my world's a little brighter these days."

I scoffed mockingly. "What a line!"

"Is it? I don't quite know how to tell you how I feel about you. If only I knew a way to express myself. I know it sounds like a line, but it's not," he said, intertwining our fingers and resting my hand in his lap while he steered the wheel with his other hand. "I've been more direct with my feelings with you than anyone in my entire life. Let's just enjoy the party and see where this takes us." He looked away but kept hold of my hand.

I stared at our palms pressing against each other. I really enjoyed being with Jack, but I was not sure if I saw a future together with him. He was so upscale, and I enjoyed life more low-key. Maybe Jack was right. I should just relax and see where this took us.

The rest of the car ride was silent, and soon, we reached the front gates of a mansion. We drove up a concrete path and stopped near a water fountain with a Greek female statue in the center. The mansion was massive with white pillars, floor-to-ceiling windows, and a pointed roof with black shingles.

The valet opened the door for me, and I stepped out, Jack came around and pulled me closer to him as we made our way inside the mansion. Many people entered through the double doors, wearing expensive jewelry and dressed in the latest fashion trends. I glanced up at Jack as he linked his arm with mine, helping me up the stairs, and I marveled at the high ceilings of the entryway. Then, we passed a painting hanging on the wall of a landscape with a lake and surrounding mountains. That was when I realized I'd catered here before.

AS I WATCHED THE GUESTS, I wondered if some of them knew my family or if a few of them were even here. The Fairfaxes were a healthy-sized family.

"Maybe I shouldn't have come. What if my father shows up?" I whispered, turning to Jack.

"He could, but you'll be fine. I'll never leave your side," he said, and I felt the weight of his words.

I allowed Jack to lead us into a large room with a massive crystal chandelier hanging above, and a grand piano with an accompanying band in the corner.

"I'm going to get us something to drink. Want to come?"

"I'll wait here," I told him, watching him disappear into the crowd.

I looked at the catering staff, wondering if anyone I knew was here. Luckily, no familiar faces showed. The moonlight shone through several windows, and rows upon rows of tables had appetizers and drinks on them. Mindless chatter and laughter filled the room, and I felt my stomach twisting.

I was so busy checking out flower arrangements that I hadn't seen Jack coming from behind me and handing me a drink.

"Victoria, meet Francis Waltham," Jack said. "He's the owner of this beautiful home."

My head whipped around, and I saw a man with a flower tucked into his blazer pocket, wearing a charming smile. "Hello," I said, reaching my hand out to shake his. "It's a pleasure to meet you."

"You as well, Ms. ..."

"Fairfax," Jack cut in. "Victoria Fairfax."

"Ah, a Fairfax! I do apologize for not inviting your grandfather to the event. I heard he's not doing well."

"I ... no, he's not," I said, feeling like I had been put on the spot. I knew nothing about my grandfather, except from what I'd read online.

"Your father, George, is a golfing buddy of mine. I haven't seen him in a while either." His eyes darted around the room before meeting mine again. "But I thought his daughter's name was Elizabeth? How is he doing?" He cast questioning eyes at me, making me feeling like I was a complete fraud.

My mouth opened and closed, and my face turned pale. I wasn't sure what to say, and I placed all of my weight on Jack.

"Francis," Jack said, "we've just arrived, and I want to introduce my date to my partners. Will you excuse us?" Jack rushed me out of the ballroom and sat me on a leather couch with intricate engravings on the wooden edges, which was pushed against the wall.

Jack left me there, only to return with a glass of water, which he handed over.

"Is this why you brought me?" I asked, looking at him crouched in front of me. I thought back to what Scarlett had said before I left. It was like she'd planted a seed in my mind. *What if Jack was only interested in me because of my estranged family?*

"What do you mean?" He appeared perplexed.

"Fairfax. I'm only here because of my name. That's why you were so eager to say it. You know I'm not connected to them, so why would you do this to me? Did you think no one would bring up my family?"

"That's not what this is at all," Jack said, pushing himself up to sit next to me. "I completely forgot that he knew the Fairfaxes. He's connected to so many people that it's hard to remember who's on his guest list. I promise, this was not to embarrass you."

"Then, why'd you say my name so quickly?" I asked, taking a slow sip of water.

"First, because it's your name, and because you were nervous, so I thought talking for you for a bit might give you time to settle in. You were distracted by everything going on, and I was trying *not* to make you feel out of place. That's what I thought anyway ..."

"I think I need some air," I expressed.

"Hold on," he said, setting down my water on a side table. "We don't have to stay long if you're uncomfortable. Just long enough for a few dances and meeting my real friends. Introducing my date to the host is always the first thing I do," he said.

Do?

I wondered how many women Jack had brought to these occasions—enough I supposed for people to think I was only the next flavor until he upgraded me for someone else. I hated thinking this way, but what did I expect?

"You just can't turn yourself off, can you? You're always looking for an angle. A way of getting new clients." I shook my head.

"I can try to turn it off," he said kindly. "For you. Just one hour, and we can walk outside. Francis has a beautiful garden."

I sighed. "Fine, but if people keep talking to me about the Fairfaxes, I'm leaving."

"Deal."

He led me back in, introducing me to more people without mentioning my last name. Most people didn't care who I was. The women were more interested in flirting with Jack, and the men just wanted to talk business. I saw a busty redhead in a black dress ogling him, but he consistently turned his focus back to me. Surprisingly, he kept every conversation short to move on to the next person. He threw in compliments about me and my work and didn't care when the guests looked down their noses. He talked about me like he was proud of who I was, and it made my heart melt.

After a while, I did feel right at home, maybe because Jack was by my side.

"Dance with me," he whispered close to my ear.

"Nope, that's not going to happen," I said, fervently shaking my head. "There is no way you're getting me out on that dance floor. You can ask that redhead, and I won't even get mad." I fluttered my fingers and shooed him away.

"What redhead?" He chuckled. Standing straight, he grabbed my hand, pulling me closer. "There is only one woman I want. One dance, and then we go for a walk. Deal?"

"Always a bargain with you," I said, letting him lead me to the dance floor.

He placed his hand on my hip and held the other one in the air, interlocked with mine. We swayed to the music, and others joined in around us. I placed my head on his chest, and I could almost feel his body heat through his shirt. It felt like magic, being held like that, and the longer we danced, the lighter I felt. Every thought in my head melted away, leaving him and me to have fun.

I felt a tickle on my ear when he leaned in and whispered, "I thought you only wanted one dance?"

"Now, I'm getting good," I said. "Maybe better than you."

He chuckled. "I've got three years of classical dance training under my belt. What do you have?"

I lifted my head from his chest and looked into his eyes. "You're lying."

"Nope. When I was a teenager, I spent an entire summer studying dance to meet girls. Turns out, ballroom dancing is actually enjoyable, so I kept it up for a while until I went to law school."

"You are just full of surprises, aren't you?" I smiled.

"Nope, no more surprises. I want you to know everything about me, Victoria." A waiter passed by with a tray of drinks, and Jack quickly snatched one to hand to me. "Let's head to the garden."

"Okay," I said, holding his hand and cuddling his arm as we walked out into the cool air. It had gotten so stuffy in there that it was nice to get out and take a breather.

We walked past short hedges in between topiaries of random shapes. The dirt path led to a garden with colorful flowers and a metal bench overlooking a small koi pond.

Jack took off his suit jacket and wrapped it over my shoulders, and we sat together on the bench, snuggling close.

"Could this guy be any more pretentious?" I asked, looking behind me at his personal golf course.

"All this garden stuff is actually because of his third wife. She had a green thumb, and I don't mean, she was a gardener. She spent money however she could, even on the most useless things, to make herself happy, but I have a feeling all this will be gone and replaced with something else when wife number four comes along,"

"Hmm, maybe I should apply for the position. He seemed very interested in my family." I tilted my head.

"Now, you can joke about it?" He nudged my side, and I nuzzled my head further into his shoulder.

"It's my family. I'm allowed to." I crossed my legs and brought his jacket closer around me.

"They're not your family," he said. "Real families stick together and are always there for you. Your father and his side of the family haven't been there for you a day in your life. You don't need them."

"What if I said I wanted ... them?" I arched my brows.

"Why?"

"My whole life, I've wanted to be a part of something bigger. I didn't need a huge house or animals cut out of leaves or fancy cars that I'd drive too fast. I just wanted to be surrounded by people who cared about me. As a kid, I had Scarlett and my brother. That was it. Don't get me wrong; they are my entire world, but sometimes, I just wish I had something more. Not a lot, just enough to fill the empty father void, I guess." I shrugged.

"What about your mom? And your stepdad, right?"

"Yeah, but he's not my stepdad. They were never legally married but have been together for years." I sighed. "My stepdad is nice, but as a kid, I thought I'd be betraying my real father if I got too close to him."

Jack wrapped his arm around my shoulders and squeezed lightly. "My parents were together for twenty years before they got divorced. My dad moved to another state, and my mom was stuck with me. I was quite the troublemaker, but I'd never have admitted that at the time."

"I'm sure you were"—I smiled—"because you still are." I stood and wobbled, slightly buzzed from the few drinks I'd had.

"I'll show you trouble," he teased, pulling me into his lap. He tightly hugged me and leaned forward.

I turned my head, and he kissed my cheek.

"Victoria ..." he said, searching my face. "Why do you keep fighting your feelings for me? What are you so afraid of? Do you think I'm that heartless that I'm going to hurt you?" Jack asked.

"You will hurt me because that's what the men in my life always do."

16

VICTORIA

"I THOUGHT I RECOGNIZED YOU," said a deep, raspy voice. "Victoria, right?"

I looked up to find Francis Waltham holding the door for me as I walked up to the hotel, carrying a box of decor. I always loved coming here, not that I could afford to stay here but Florence Catering had plenty of events I worked at either as a server or bartender. The hotel was prestigious, and maybe my love for this place came from a mischief fictional character I adored as a child. The Plaza Hotel served as a backdrop to Kay Thompson's *Eloise* about a girl who lived in the penthouse.

"Oh ... Mr. Waltham. Hi. What are you doing here?" I peered around him thinking I might find Jack with him since I knew they had lunch together often, but he wasn't there.

"I had a meeting with a client," he told me. "But I'm surprised to find you here."

"I'm preparing a bridal party," I said, showing him the box.

His eyes slightly widened. "Oh, Jack didn't tell me. Congratulations. When is the wedding?"

"Oh no, we're—" I shook my head, feeling the heat rising in the back of my neck.

"I'm glad you're able to work things out, and ready to take your relationship to the next level."

What was he talking about?

"No, Jack and I—" I tried to clarify.

"When I first found out that Jack was taking on the case and dating his client's daughter I thought it could only be a recipe for disaster. I even told him so."

"Told him what?" I blinked.

"Not to work on a case against your mother," he said.

My what?

"Sorry, I'm not following?" I frowned. "Jack and I are not engaged."

He realized something, and suddenly, he was at a loss for words. "Oh. You meant, a client's bridal shower." He shut his eyes for a split second. "I'm such an idiot. It slipped my mind. Yes, Jack told me about your new venture in the catering business. How is it going?"

What just happened? What case against my mother?

"It's keeping me busy," I said.

His gaze went down to the box. "Here, let me help you with that." He pulled the box from my hands.

"Thank you," I replied.

"Lead the way." He smiled, following me inside the building and down the lobby.

We walked into a room where a few of my staff were placing chairs around the tables. We had been at it since early this morning, preparing for the bridal shower of Jack's partner's daughter, which was supposed to start at noon. Jack had been very supportive, and thanks to him, I had several of his acquaintances booking me to plan their next parties.

"You could set it on that table." I pointed to the one in the corner.

"You should give me your business card. I have a few events next year that I could use your services for."

"Yes, of course. That would be great." I reached into my purse and pulled out one of my cards.

He looked down at it, and as his eyes met mine, something in his face changed. "Before ... what I said, it was a mistake. I had confused you with someone else."

"Oh, right. Sure, don't worry about it." I coolly waved my hands in the air, but inside, I couldn't shake off the fact that he had said something important. Something I should know.

LATER THAT NIGHT, I glanced at Jack sitting on my couch and then walked into my room to change and grab my purse.

"What restaurant are you taking me to?" I called out to Jack.

We were alone. Scarlett was working, and even though she had told me she was happy for me, I never really felt that.

"I'd suggest you change into something more relaxed ... if that's why you're asking," Jack said from the other room.

"Perfect, just what I had in mind," I said, coming back out, wearing slim jeans and a lightweight crew neck sweater. "Are you ready to go?"

As we walked downstairs, Jack held my hand. He guided me to where his Cadillac was parked.

"I saw your friend today," I said.

"Yeah, who?"

"Francis Waltham, and he said the weirdest thing," I said, watching him closely.

"Like what?"

"He said he told you not to take the case ... against my mother. What do you think he was talking about?" I asked.

Jack's jaw clenched, his eyes sweeping over his car.

"What lawsuit is there against my mother?" I urged him on for an answer.

I cast a glance up at him, trying to read him, but Jack was good at concealing things. *What would Jack have to do with my mother?* Maybe Francis had had me confused with someone else. At least, I hoped.

"I have no idea what he's talking about, Victoria. I'm not the only lawyer he's acquainted with. Are you starving? Because I'm famished," he said, opening the door for me to get into his car.

I accepted his answer even though my gut was telling me something else.

When I slipped inside, I braced myself, but shockingly, he didn't speed. He went the exact speed limit and sometimes slower when the traffic was heavy.

"What's going on?" I asked. "Forgot where the gas pedal is?" I arched my brow.

He turned and smirked. "I've noticed how you tense up every time you're in the car with me."

"How much is it killing you?" I knew Jack had a heavy foot on the gas pedal.

"I'm dying an excruciating death on the inside."

I laughed. "Well, thank you for your consideration."

"Can a man be dangerous and sexy, even playing it safe?"

I scrunched my nose. "No, unless you want me to call you old man."

"Well then, I definitely don't want you to call me that." He added some pressure to the metal, and the car picked up speed.

"Talking about grandfathers ... was mine really that big of a deal?" I asked as I looked out the window.

"He still is," he said. "It's too bad you can't have a piece of the legacy."

I shrugged. "I will make my own legacy."

"There's no doubt about that," Jack added.

We exchanged a flirty glance, and then I fiddled with the car radio, knowing something deep down was still bothering me. I couldn't find anything I liked, so I turned it off. Ten minutes later, we were parked, and I was about to get out of the car.

"Wait," he said, placing his hand on my thigh. He turned my head toward him and planted a kiss on my lips.

"It doesn't matter if you're a Fairfax or not, rich or poor, as long as you're mine," Jack said, looking deep in my eyes.

When I pulled away, I smiled at him. "Is this your way of asking me to be your girlfriend?"

"I've never been a traditional guy. Go with it." He kissed me again before getting out of his car and walked around to open the door for me.

I held on to his arm as we entered the restaurant. It was packed, and I wondered how long we'd have to wait to get a table.

As I was about to bring this up to Jack, the host smiled at us and said, "Mr. Turner! How lovely to see you again. Who's this lovely woman you've brought with you tonight?"

"Antoine, this is my girlfriend, Victoria," he said with pride in his voice, and it made my heart melt.

"Pleasure." The man smiled and ushered us forward, and we weaved through the tables toward one in the middle, which sat on a lower level than the front of the restaurant.

The host pulled the chair out and helped me settle in. Then, he placed the menus on the table. Jack sat down and opened his menu. I stared at him with thin lips, trying not to fall in love with the man. We had been seeing each other now for several weeks, and even though things were amazing between us, I couldn't help feeling that the bottom of the box would fall out any minute. Finally, Jack looked up and caught my disappointed expression.

"What's going on?" he asked. "I'm buying, so don't worry about it."

"That's not what I'm worried about," I said, fiddling with my bracelet.

"Then, what?"

Jack placed his menu down and just kept looking at me with those thoughtful eyes. He wasn't trying to yank my chain or make moves just to sleep with me. I knew Jack genuinely wanted to be with me, but yet I couldn't help feeling like something just wasn't right.

"Are you still thinking about what Francis said earlier?" he asked, and I nodded. "Forget about it, and let's focus on what we are doing now."

"And what are you doing now?" I placed my elbow on the table and rested my chin in my palm.

"I'm trying to have a nice dinner with my beautiful girlfriend."

"Maybe I should call my mother ..." I reached for my purse. "Maybe she knows something."

"Victoria," he said, reaching across the table to grab my hand. "Stop looking for things that don't exist. He made a mistake. Let's focus on us and enjoy each other's company."

I slowly picked up my menu and looked at him over the top of it. He was right. I needed to lighten up and not be so suspicious. I still couldn't help myself. My gut was telling me there was something Jack wasn't saying. My heart was so conflicted, and I wasn't sure if I would be able to enjoy myself at all.

———————

WHEN DESSERT CAME, I sensed that he had something

important to tell me. He didn't touch the cake and kept fiddling with his napkin. There was something solemn about him.

"Should we call it a night?" I asked.

He looked up at me, confused. "You haven't finished the cake."

"I can't eat this by myself." I leaned into my chair, feeling full.

He half-smiled and stabbed the corner with his fork. Popping it into his mouth, he continued with the same serious demeanor. "There's been something weighing on my mind. I want to tell you because I know how important it is that I don't keep secrets. I'm just not sure how to tell you this."

"What? You look like you're about to tell me you're actually married," I mused, and his expression remained stony. My smile faded. "You're not married, right?"

"No, don't be silly." He chuckled.

"Whatever it is, just tell me."

"There's something you should know, and after what I tell you, I wouldn't blame you if you never wanted to see me again." He looked down at his hands, and I began to worry.

"We had a history … Luke's mom and me. We dated back at Harvard, but we remained friends, even after she got married."

"Okay … why are you telling me this?" I frowned.

"Why do you think?" he said, and I shifted in my chair. "I care about you, Victoria, and whatever this is between us, it can't start on lies," he said.

His words went right through me, and my pulse began to pick up.

"What I'm about to tell you, I've never told anyone before … I'm not Luke's godfather." His eyes met mine.

"You're not?" I frowned. "So, you've been lying to me?"

"No, that's true; I am. But I'm also his biological father."

Did I hear that right?

"You're his ... Luke's father?" I shook my head in disbelief.

I had met Luke's father once—tall, blond, and definitely wasn't a lawyer.

But Jack?

"Colleen, Luke's mother, had been separated at the time when we had a one-night stand ... or rekindled our relationship. Anyway, that's not important, but after a week, she got back with her husband, and I was left out of the equation." He placed his napkin on the table. "A month later, she told me she was pregnant, and the baby was mine."

I leaned back in my chair, stunned by the new revelation.

"Luke didn't know, did he?" I asked.

When he didn't answer, my heart flattened.

"Only Colleen and me ... and, now, you," Jack said.

I looked at him in disbelief. *Why was he telling me this, trusting me with this gigantic secret?*

"I don't understand why you didn't want to claim him as yours." I felt the anger rising inside me. I knew what it was like to be cast aside by your own father. "You refused to own up and acknowledge the existence of your own son. Do you know how much I would kill to be part of my father's life and his legacy? To feel like I'm part of a loving family? The moment you chose to lie, you took something from that little boy. You took away part of his identity. Everything was a lie to him. How could you do that?"

I saw the light go out from his eyes.

"Believe me, Victoria, I torture myself every day about what could have been if I'd told the truth from the start. I could have been raising my son, but I did what was right for Luke. Colleen had three older children and no desire to raise Luke as ours." His shoulders dropped. "And I ... what could I offer Luke? I didn't want to break up her family. So, I did the only thing I could and allowed another man to raise my son."

"That is so sad." I saw another side of Jack, a disheartened one.

Jack always seemed so guarded, and now, I knew why. It must have been hard for Jack to take the backseat in Luke's life, especially when he stood in the distance, witnessing Luke's health deteriorating.

I knew what it was like to have a father completely refusing to acknowledge that you existed. But Jack had found a way to be in his life, even with the circumstances. I had to give him credit for that.

"I carry this unbearable guilt that I denied my son from ever knowing the truth, and now, I have to live with it for the rest of my life. You know now. I'm a horrible person, and you should stay away from me."

He glanced down at me. In a way, I wished I could kiss him, but I didn't. Instead, I took his hand in mine.

"He was an angel, and I didn't deserve to be in his life," he said with a heavy sigh.

"No," I snapped and then gave him an apologetic glance. "No, Jack. At the end of the day, you loved him, and Luke loved you. That's what matters."

"I'm not any better than your father." He diverted his eyes away from me.

"You can't compare yourself to my father. He's never been there for me, not like you were there for Luke," I said, waiting for the tears to burn my eyes, but I didn't allow myself. I had run out of tears long ago for my father.

"Have you ever thought about contacting your father?"

I let out a long breath. "That's a heavy question, Jack. Sure, a big part of me wants to, but after everything my mother told me about him, I don't want someone who doesn't want me in their life."

"What if your mother was wrong? I mean, I'm not saying

your mother is a liar, but what if she only told you half of the story?"

I shifted to get a better look at Jack. "Do you know something I don't?"

He hesitated before saying, "I wish I could tell you if I did." He ran his finger over my hand, and it put me in a trance.

I sighed. "We're a couple of messed up people, aren't we? I guess we have more in common than I thought."

"It's not the kind of things I want to have in common with you, but I don't want secrets between us," he said, wrapping his hand around mine. "We both have a past that we can't change, and we're angry from everything we've suffered. I believe that we were brought together for a reason."

"And you think Luke is the reason?" I asked.

"I like to think so." He smiled a little. "I need a break ... away from here and work. You want to come to Vermont with me?"

I laughed.

"I'm serious. Let's escape. Get out of town over the weekend. You and me."

"My schedule isn't exactly nine to five, especially with my business now. I have a few clients I need to meet to finalize the menu for their upcoming parties. And, not to mention, you've got clients who are counting on you," I said.

"The beauty of being name partner is that I can delegate my work whenever I want. Plus, there're these magical things called phones. Did you know you could check e-mails on it? And talk to people anywhere in the world?"

"All right, smart-ass. I don't know. Let me think about it." I smiled teasingly.

"There's a pool," he grinned, leaning back in his seat, staring at me.

"Oh, a chance to see you in your swimming trunks?"

"See what you could be missing." He smirked. "So, we're doing this?"

"Okay. Just give me a chance and see what I can do about my schedule, and I'll let you know for sure."

"When you do, I'll get my assistant to set everything up, and then I'll come get you on Friday."

"Sounds like a plan," I said.

"Should I get you home now?" he asked.

"Want to go for a walk? I don't want to go home just yet."

After a short pause, Jack said, "You don't hate me, Victoria?"

I lifted my eyes to his and said, "I never want to hate you again."

17

VICTORIA

I KNEW I SHOULDN'T, but I told Scarlett everything. I couldn't keep something like this to myself. I needed a friend to talk to, and Scarlett was good at keeping secrets.

We sat on the couch with wineglasses and a tube of cookie dough, like we used to do in college. It was something we hadn't done in a while. It felt nice to be us again.

"I still can't believe that," Scarlett said. "What are the chances that you'd be in similar situations? And that everything revolves around Luke. It's like it was ..."

"Don't say fate."

"But it's true. What if you had gone to a different hospital to volunteer? What if you'd never worked the animal shelter or the event in the park? All of these things brought you closer to Jack, and now, he wants you to go to Vermont of all places. That's the most romantic place to go," she said.

I'd told her that Jack had invited me on a trip to Vermont. I had been hesitant at first because I didn't want to hurt her feelings. But she'd been seeing someone from work and seemed to be over it. I was relieved that we could put all this tension between us behind and move on with our lives.

"I beg to differ. Are you forgetting about Paris?"

"Oh crap," Scarlett said, setting down her wineglass. "Speaking of Paris, I have something for you ..." She stood and ran to the kitchen to grab a big orange envelope addressed to me. "This came by courier while you were gone. I hope you're not mad."

"Mad?" I stared at the return address, which said *International School of Culinary Arts*. "What is this? Why would I get mail from them?" I sat up, looking at Scarlett, who settled beside me with a guilty look on her face. "Scar?"

"Right, um ... remember when you were supposed to fill out the application, and then when Luke died, you changed your mind? Well, I filled out an application in your name and sent it out to a school."

"What?"

"I'm so sorry. Please don't hate me. I know the tuition is a killer, and you're not ready for school, so don't feel like you have to do anything."

"Scar, this was over a year ago. Why would I just be getting a package from them now? It's probably junk."

"Their waitlist is crazy since they're such a highly coveted school. Maybe they're looking for new applicants and saw your name."

"This is nothing," I said, tossing the package on the table.

Scarlett turned to face me and looked deep into my eyes.

"Okay, it's creepy when you stare at me like that." I diverted my eyes to my wineglass.

"Then, stop being an idiot! Do you remember when we were applying for colleges? Most of mine were rejection letters that came in very flat envelopes while yours came in bulky envelopes from schools practically begging you to wear their colors. I promise you, this envelope is an acceptance letter to that school."

"I don't know ..."

I had considered applying over a year ago when I read an article in a magazine about the program. I had never wanted to be a chef, but I thought the experience would bring a set of skills that would benefit my catering firm.

"Just open it!" Scarlett chucked it in my lap.

"You're so pushy," I groaned, slowly running my nail under the tab to open it. I dumped out the package and unfolded the letter at the top.

"*Dear Ms. Fairfax,*

"*We're delighted to inform you that we're extending an offer for you to join our fall program. You'll be among a group of ten students who have piqued our interest but have not been formally accepted as a full-time student. Please accept this offer at your earliest convenience once you have reviewed the informational packet enclosed,*" I read out loud. My smile widened with each new word and my voice increased in pitch.

"It's going to be an experience of a lifetime!" Scarlett shouted, wrapping her arms around me. "What else does it say?"

"It goes on to talk about the scholarship opportunities and the potential to earn work after the program is done." I glanced up and met her emerald eyes.

"Why don't you look more thrilled about that?"

"It's a great opportunity," I sighed. "But I don't know if I could leave my whole life behind."

"Seriously? It's only six months," she gasped. "Your life will be here, waiting for you, when you get back."

"There's also ... never mind." I huffed.

Scarlett rolled her eyes and sprawled across the couch with her head in my lap. "You're smart enough not to give up a dream because of a boy."

"Jack is not a boy," I said.

But she was right; this was an unexpected opportunity.

"You'll have plenty of time to hang out with him after the program is done. If he loves you, then he'll wait."

Then, it crossed my mind. Jack never said he loved me. I mean, I always assumed he did by his actions, but he never said those words out loud.

"I don't know if I can go. I'd feel like I was abandoning him, and after everything he told me about being Luke's father, I don't want him to think it's an excuse to run away."

"This is your dream. You have your catering business to think about. Who knows? Maybe you'll like it there and stay. You think they don't need catering businesses in France?"

"Maybe ... I wish it hadn't happened all at the same time. We just started seeing each other, and I know a long-distance relationship will put a strain on us." I took a sip from my glass.

"Or maybe he'll move there with you," Scarlett said, and I glanced down at her.

"That's highly unlikely," I refuted.

I felt a strong connection to Jack, one that I'd never felt with anyone before. But I knew Jack would never leave everything he'd worked so hard for behind in New York to go across the world for me. And not that I would want him to sacrifice his life. Anyhow, I was getting way ahead of myself. I wasn't sure I wanted to go even though it was a great opportunity. I had changed drastically since Luke died, and maybe, now, I wanted something else. A chance with Jack.

"*Oh*," Scarlett said solemnly, sitting up and resting her head on the top of the couch. "I see what this is really about." Her eyelashes fluttered.

"What do you mean?"

"You think you're helping Jack find his closure. That's not your responsibility, Vicky. It's Jack's problem and Luke's mother.

You did your part to make Luke comfortable in the hospital, and you can't let his death be what holds you back. Nothing should hold you back."

"It's not about them. It's a big decision." And, now, I just didn't know how it was going to fit in with Jack. Long-distance relationships usually didn't last.

"I think you should go for it—or, at the very least, talk to Jack about it and see what he thinks. He'll probably tell you the same thing I am. You would be foolish not to go."

"You're right; I will talk to him. When the time is right," I told her.

18

VICTORIA

WHEN WE GOT to the runway, my first instinct was to send pictures to Scarlett, but I was too busy admiring the plane. As Jack helped me up the stairs, I was in awe at the luxurious decor and the flight attendants who would cater to our every need. One could get used to this kind of lifestyle. I sat in the white leather chair and looked out on the tarmac.

"I can't believe you own a plane," I chimed.

"It's a perk," he said casually.

I watched as Jack settled in the seat in front of me.

One of the female flight attendants walked up to me and smiled. "Can I get you anything to drink, miss?"

"No, thank you," I said, lifting my eyes to Jack. "Is the flight long?"

"A little over an hour," Jack hummed. "Sometimes, I wonder if it's longer to get the plane ready than to travel there."

"You go there often?"

"No, actually. One of the potential clients that my firm was hoping to take on lived there. He was dealing with family issues, but we wanted him so bad that I flew back and forth, taking meeting after meeting."

"Did you end up getting him as a client?" I asked.

"He refused our deal to go to our competitor. Either way, it's a beautiful state, and I'm glad I got to make the trips."

"I guess you don't always get your way," I teased.

"You realize I said, my firm. If I wanted his business, then I would have gotten it. But the guy was a total douche bag, and I have my limits with who I want to deal with," he said. "It's not always about making money, Victoria."

"So, what is it about?" My eyes trailed around the cabin.

Whatever he was doing, he was doing a pretty good job at it.

"It's about being a man with integrity. In my line of work, I don't want to be just good at what I'm doing. I want to be a legend." He flashed me a smile.

Jack wore confidence well, making him appear sexier. But, in my eyes, I knew there was more to him. Jack had a heart. He had funded the bookstore with a learning center for kids with disabilities and had opened a charity in Luke's name. He cared about people, and that was what I found sexy in Jack Turner.

I flipped through the magazines and books on the table. Most of them were about business, so I decided to close my eyes instead. When I felt someone watching me, I slowly opened my lids to find Jack staring at me.

"You're some kind of beautiful, aren't you?" he said, making the heat rise to my cheeks.

I lifted my head up. "You're not going to get obsessed with me, Jack, are you?"

"I can't promise you anything." He smiled, and my heart fluttered.

When we got to our destination, I was loaded into another town car to go to the resort.

I was excited to be here with Jack. I had never been to Vermont before, and there was so much beautiful scenery to view. The car dropped us off in front of the lobby, and a bellboy instantly unloaded our bags for us. Jack put his hand on the small of my back and guided me into the hotel. The decor was rustic, almost like it was a ranch but one hundred times the size. He explained that it had a pool and a gym as we walked up to the reception desk.

Behind the desk was a woman dressed in a blue blazer and black pantsuit. Her blonde hair flowed down her shoulders, and a gold necklace dangled from her neck. She typed on her keyboard, quickly looking up at us. "Welcome to the Evergreen Resort and Spa. How may I help you?" she asked cheerfully. When she looked up and saw Jack, her smile vanished. "Oh, Mr. Turner, nice to see you again," she said, but the tone sounded off.

"Hello, Molly. I'm just checking in," Jack said.

I caught the icy gaze on the receptionist's face and then Jack's smirk.

What was I missing?

As I felt the tension between them, Molly gave Jack the key card, and when he grabbed it, she held it tightly between her thumb and finger.

"Hope you enjoy your stay," she said, gritting her teeth before letting us leave.

"How do you two know each other?" I asked, walking beside him.

"What do you mean?" He frowned, casting a look my way.

"It was evident she was pissed at you ... and you knew her by name."

"That's very observant, but she had a name tag on." He walked up to the elevator and pushed the button.

"True, but ... the way she was acting with you made me think you knew each other."

"I don't know what you're talking about," he declared, chest expanded.

"You had a fling . . . and you never called her back, right?"

I didn't take my eyes off him, waiting for the doors to open. He didn't look at me or say a word.

Entering the elevator, I was still met with silence. I was trying not to be a jealous girlfriend, and I knew Jack had had many affairs in the past. I either accepted it or not, but either way, he was entitled to his past—as long it didn't endanger our future together.

We made it to our room with a king-size bed that had a luxury bathroom. There was a balcony looking out to a vast field of trees. The room came equipped with a fridge and microwave. I had been hoping for a stove to cook on, but I figured Jack would mostly want to order in or go out.

"Are you going to tell me what that was about?" I was curious now, not jealous. Or at least, that was what I kept telling myself.

He stood there for a second with his hands in his pockets, grinning, and it was infuriating to me that he wasn't saying anything.

"You keep saying you want no secrets between us, but then things like this keep happening. What's your deal?" I debated.

Jack kicked off his shoes and sprawled out on the bed. He patted the spot beside him, and we snuggled close together.

"I didn't think it was important enough to talk about, and it happened a year ago."

"What did?" I raised my brow.

"Are you sure you want to go down this road? You might regret hearing the whole story."

"I want to know." I lifted my chin up to look down at him.

He sighed deeply before saying, "I did something I really regret. The last time I came to this place, Molly gave me the key to my room. I was in a hurry, so I went up and found the door open. I dropped off my luggage and left to go see my client," he said with a smile, knowing this was not what I'd imagined.

I was such an idiot.

"But, when I came back and went into my room, my suitcase and files were all gone," he said.

"That's weird!"

"Unfortunately, I directed my anger toward poor Molly." His lips thinned out. "It wasn't my finest moment, I'll admit. It wasn't her fault, and she did try to locate my stuff. It's just ... so much crap was going on in my life." He rubbed his eyes, and it made me believe it might have been around the time Luke died.

"Did you end up finding your luggage?"

"Yep. I had placed them in the wrong room, and I felt terrible for taking it out on her. I apologized afterward, but I guess I'll never get back in her good graces."

"Oh, so that's what it was." I yawned. "I think I'm going to make myself a coffee. Would you like—"

"Oh." He mimicked a high-pitched tone and rolled me on my back. "Not so fast," he said, looking down at me, pinning me underneath him.

The heat rose inside me.

"What did you think? I had a fling with Molly?" He chuckled.

"I—"

Yes, I did.

"You're cute when you're jealous."

"I wasn't! I was just curious; that's all," I blurted.

"You have nothing to be jealous about. I'm here with you, and I want only you." His heated eyes trailed the length of me, and my breath caught in my throat. "When are you going to understand that?" He had never looked at me like that before—so loving. He leaned in closer, and deepened his kiss before pulling up.

160

"I have an idea," he said. "Why don't we put all this energy you have into a swim?"

I smiled. "Now?"

"Go put on your bathing suit or hiking boots. I'm good with either."

"But I didn't bring hiking boots." I frowned, tracing the outline of his face, down to the Y-shaped fissure on his chin, taking a moment to appreciate how gorgeous this man was. And he was all mine.

"Sneakers are fine too." He smiled, and my eyes went down to the opening of his V-neck, which revealed a nicely toned upper body.

What are we talking about?

"What if I want to go swimming?" I looked up at him through my eyelashes.

"Then, put on a bathing suit. Aren't you following the conversation?" He nuzzled my neck, and I got the strong scent of his sweet cologne.

I couldn't focus on anything right now. I forced myself to pull away.

"Okay, I'll change, but you have to come in, too."

"Can't I just watch you?" He smiled mischievously.

"Looky-loos are not appreciated," I said, laughing and pushing him off.

I glanced back, and Jack was lying on his back, his hands behind his head. I couldn't resist and found myself going back to him, kissing him long and hard.

"Go and get ready," he groaned. "Before I change my mind."

I got up, laughing.

I rifled through my suitcase and then slinked into the bathroom to change. It was a black one-piece with straps that crossed at the back. I slipped into matching flip-flops and wrapped a sarong around me. When I exited the bathroom, Jack wasn't there.

"Jack?" I called out.

I heard a voice on the terrace. Looking through the window, I saw he was on his phone, jaw clenched and pacing back and forth. I went behind the curtain and brought my ear closer to the opening of the patio door. He was talking to someone, but I couldn't hear the words.

When I walked back to my suitcase, Jack opened the door slightly, covering the speaker of his phone, and said, "It's a business call. I promise I'm almost done, okay? I'll be back in a bit."

"Sure." I grinned, knowing this was what it must be like to be with Jack.

His career took up most of his life, and if I wanted to be with him, I had to accept that.

I launched myself onto the bed on my stomach, feeling the soft blankets. Checking my phone that I'd left on the nightstand, I saw two missed calls and a bunch of texts from Scarlett.

I responded with, *Arrived safe. See you Monday!* and a heart emoji.

Jack entered the room and gently closed the door. He leaned against it and smiled. "What a lovely view."

"You won't get to see it much longer if you don't change." I said.

After a few minutes, I looked up and he was still standing there. "I thought we were going swimming."

"Sorry, I get so easily distracted by your ... beauty."

It was corny, but I blushed anyway. "Keep saying things like that, and I might have to kiss you again." I got off the bed and placed my phone on the nightstand.

"Why look for an excuse? I give you carte blanche. Feel free to do it whenever the urge arises." He chuckled.

I smiled and stood on my tiptoes to wrap my arms around his

neck. Gently, I pressed my lips against his, and my body tingled. He grabbed my hips and ran his hands up and down my back and through my hair. Pushing him away, I sat back on the bed.

"Bathing suit. Now. Do I need to bring a towel?"

"They have everything down there," he said before disappearing through the bathroom door to get ready to go.

WHEN WE GOT to the pool, I pushed open the glass door and entered the cool night air. I kicked off my shoes and sarong to dip my feet. It was warm and tingly against my skin as Jack sat at the edge of the pool with his feet dangling in.

"Aren't you going in?"

"The water is cold. I need time to work myself in," Jack said.

Suddenly, I pushed Jack in and made a huge splash.

He surfaced, pushing his hair out of his face. "Are you sure that's how you want to play it?"

I shrugged playfully. "You set yourself up for it. Who sits on the edge of the pool without jumping in?"

"Lots of people!" He swam to the edge and propped his elbows up on the ledge.

"Are you coming, or do I have to come and get you?" he said in a husky voice that made me tingle inside.

As I got in the water, Jack wasted no time to pull me closer to him. "You didn't want to dive in?"

"I'm not the strongest swimmer, and I hate diving. Gives me a weird feeling in my stomach." I kissed his cheek and was about to push off the wall to the other side when he grabbed my hand.

"I know how you can relax."

"I'm already quite relaxed," I smiled.

He tucked my hair behind my ear and then kissed my lips. He held me close before wrapping one arm under my legs and the other under my back. He carried me to the shallow end, and I giggled.

"What are you doing?"

"Helping you relax. I can feel your muscles tensing up by the second. Be a starfish."

I raised my eyebrows and laughed. "When I said I wasn't a strong swimmer, I didn't mean I didn't know how to swim. This is kid stuff. I'm not going to do the starfish."

"Be a starfish, and I'll give you a hint about my surprise tomorrow night."

"Ooh, what kind of surprise?" I asked, arching a brow, "Maybe we could make a game out of it instead? I'll guess, and if you get it right, you have to tell me."

"That's never going to happen. My original deal to you will expire in three ... two ..."

"Okay, okay!" I said, stretching out my arms and legs.

He supported my back and helped me float down to the center of the pool.

"How are you feeling now?" he asked.

"Peaceful," I said, listening to the gentle slosh of the water as he moved me. "It's so quiet here that it's almost like we're the only ones staying at the resort."

"This is nice ... me and you," he said.

I fluttered my eyes open, allowing my feet to touch the floor. He brought me into his arms and looked me in the eyes.

"You never talk about yourself, do you?" he asked.

"I would rather listen than to talk," I said, wrapping my arms around him. "What is it you want to know?"

"Does it bother you that I'm older then you?"

This was the first time we'd ever talked about our age gap. Not that ten years made much of a difference, not to me anyway.

I blinked. "Does it bother you?"

"No," he said like it wasn't an afterthought.

"So, why should I care about age? What's important is that you care about me and treat me right. And I promise to repay the favor." I smiled, wrapping my arms around his neck.

"That, you never have to worry about," he replied.

I kissed his lips before I swam to get out of the pool. Grabbing a towel from the canvas pool chair, I dried myself. Suddenly, Jack was hugging me from behind and kissing my neck.

"Why don't we go get some rest?" I asked. "But, first, what's my clue?"

He thought about it for a minute and then said, "It's something you have to dress casual for."

"We're going on a nature walk tomorrow?" I guessed, remembering he'd asked me to put on my hiking boots.

"Yes, but the surprise won't happen there."

19

VICTORIA

THE NEXT DAY, we spent the whole day hiking and then went back to the room to get ready. Jack was taking me out to dinner, and I had no idea what this surprise was supposed to be.

Could it be possible he was going to propose? I let out a low laugh.

No, it was impossible. We barely knew each other, but he'd been acting odd all day—nervous, I would say. *But what if he did?* I still hadn't decided if I was going to Paris or when I should tell Jack if I did. I wanted both, but I knew it wouldn't be possible. If I did go, then I felt like I'd be abandoning New York with unsettled business, but I was trying to convince myself otherwise. It was a great opportunity. I'd miss Scarlett; however, I knew I could easily make new friends, but what about Jack?

He is irreplaceable.

"Are you almost ready to go?" Jack asked.

"Not yet," I called out from the bathroom.

I checked the mirror one more time to see if my red lipstick was out of place, and when I walked out, I found Jack patiently waiting by the front door.

He whistled as his eyes took me in. "I'm one lucky man."

"Oh, before I forget, I got you something," I said, pulling out a keychain of a tiny Vermont license plate. I had customized the word *Hotshot* in middle.

"Cute." He chuckled. "When did you get this?"

"When you were on a business call, I went downstairs to browse around the small boutiques in the lobby," I said. "It's not much, but I just thought it would make you laugh."

"Thank you," he said, allowing his fingers to play with the tips of my hair.

"It's really nothing, Jack." It surprised me how taken he was over a little keychain. The man had everything, for heaven's sake.

"It's not nothing. You thought about me." He leaned in and kissed me. "I'm sorry if my work keeps getting in the way," he said, sliding his arms around my waist. "My career is a big part of who I am."

"I know. You don't need to explain." I went in for another quick kiss. "Shall we go? I'm so curious to know what this surprise is."

"I just hope you like it."

"Why wouldn't I?" I asked, but something in his eyes had me worried.

MINUTES LATER, we headed out of the lobby and into a rental car. Jack drove us to a little restaurant about ten minutes away from the hotel.

Inside the restaurant, the hostess led us to the empty table, and Jack paused, giving me an odd look.

"What's the matter?" I asked.

He rubbed his jawline. "Nothing ..." he said without meeting my eyes. "Um, give me a sec. I need to make a call. I'll be right back," he said, and I nodded.

I placed my black clutch purse on the table and sat down. The waiter came around and poured me a glass of wine—something Jack had ordered, no doubt. I took a sip from my glass, and my eyes peered around the room. It was quiet for a Sunday night. Actually, there was no one, except for us and the staff.

When Jack returned five minutes later, he had a smile on his face but the kind like he was hiding something. *Agitation?*

"What is this surprise? What did you do?" I asked.

He smiled. His stoic demeanor excited me further. We were getting closer to whatever it was. I could feel it.

"Nothing risqué," he said, but his voice was a little off, making me believe otherwise. "You're just going to have to wait and see."

I watched Jack's eyes go up above my head, and as I turned, there he was.

George Fairfax—my father.

"Hello, Victoria."

I jolted back to Jack, and my heart stopped. I had never met the man face-to-face, but I had Googled him far too many times to know what he looked like.

"Do you know who I am?" George asked.

"Of course I do. What are you doing here?" I frowned.

My father was a stranger. I kept reminding myself. And, obviously, so was Jack. I couldn't believe he had done this to me. This setup was no doubt something that would benefit him.

"Surprise," Jack said.

When I finally allowed my eyes to meet Jack's, his smile faded.

What had he been thinking, putting me in this situation without asking me if I wanted to be here to begin with?

"Jack," I said, my throat tightening up.

Jack held his hand up. "Before you say anything, just hear me out. I invited your father for dinner—"

"To Vermont?" I said flatly.

It was a known fact that my father had a second home in Vermont, but I would never have imagined I'd be deceived like this, and my heart took a dive. Jack had had it all planned out. This was the only reason we were here, not because he wanted to spend a couple of days with me, and I felt utterly betrayed.

"Have an open mind, and just listen to what he has to say. That's all I ask."

Jack got up, and I flashed him a pleading look not to leave me alone with my father.

"I'll allow you two to catch up." Jack walked over, whispering in my ear, "I won't be far." He kissed my head and left.

What was he thinking? I was an adult. *Why would I need my father now? Where was he all those times when I needed comforting, when I needed my father in my life?*

"May I?" George pointed to the empty chair in front of me, and I was too speechless and furious that I could only nod. "Nice little place," he said, smiling.

My lips thinned out. I glanced across the table at the man sitting in front of me. We had the same color eyes and the prominent cheekbones, and I wondered if he was as stubborn as I was.

"It's been a long time."

No kidding.

"After twenty-five years, now, you're here to play catch-up?" I shrugged my shoulders. "What was this supposed to be, a happy reunion? Are we supposed to uncover things about each other? Do you want to know my hobbies? How about if we share the same taste in music?" I said in a rush.

"Victoria, I know you're upset, and you have every right to be. Let me explain, please. Then, if you don't want to see me again, I'll respect that, okay?"

I sat back in my chair and gave a slight nod for him to continue.

"I've done so many things in my life that I regret. You were never one of them," he said.

As the words came out of his mouth, my heart wanted to believe him, but my gut was whispering something else.

"So, why did you walk out on me?" I asked. "Why haven't you tried to contact me all these years?"

"I would like to tell you all about it, but the simplest answer is, your mother forced me out of your life."

"I don't believe you." I crossed my arms.

"When we were married, she suspected I had been cheating on her, and she hired a detective to follow me around." He sighed deeply. "In her possession, she has these pictures and videos ... evidence that she threatened to go to the media with. She's been holding them over my head for years, using it to blackmail me out of seeing you or for more money."

"What? Impossible," I scoffed.

"Go ahead and ask her," he demanded. "Who do you think has supported you and your family all these years? Your mother? She's barely worked a day in her life."

My mother couldn't work since she had my brother. Being in and out of hospitals had made it impossible for her to keep a steady job. But then she would come back from her Vegas trips with her boyfriend, claiming they'd won big. *Could it be that they had been extorting my father?*

I felt a burning sensation at the bottom of my stomach. *Could it be true?*

"I'm sorry to be the one to tell you this, but your mother is a gold-digger. My father is on his deathbed as we speak, and she's blackmailing me for half of my inheritance."

I had always been desperately searching for a sense of identity, something to belong to, a family. But this was not the way I wanted to meet my father, and now, he was trying to take whatever little I had away—by destroying whatever love I had with my mother.

"What do you want from me?" My eyes met his straight on.

"I want you to convince your mother to drop the case and turn over whatever she has on me." He paused. "I'll make it worth your time," George said, resting his hands on the table.

"What does that even mean? Money?" I raised my eyebrows.

He reached inside his suit pocket and pulled out a pen and a check. "Name your price."

I couldn't believe it. This was a setup, and he was bribing me —his daughter.

"What if she refuses?" I raised my brows, holding tight to the edge of the table.

"Well then ... the deal is off."

I blinked. "Wow, you're something else, aren't you? This is why you brought me here? You couldn't care less about me." I leaned back into my chair, deflated.

The small spark of hope went out like a candle. He wasn't here for me, not at all, and I was heartbroken. *Again.*

"Well, your time is up!" I said, slowly rising. "Don't contact me, and I hope I never see your face again."

Picking up my purse from the table, I turned to leave. On my way out, I asked the hostess to call me a cab because, with the way my blood was boiling, there was no way I was going to get back in the car with Jack. As far as I was concerned, it was over between us.

Outside, I heard my name being called out, but I just kept on walking toward the parking lot. I only stopped when Jack pulled on my arm.

"Where are you going?" Jack asked.

I spun around to face him. "Home to New York."

"What's going on?"

"Don't act coy with me, Jack. You planned this whole thing, didn't you? How much was he paying you, huh?"

"What are you talking about?" His forehead furrowed.

"George. How much did you get to bring me here?"

His eyes bored into me. "I don't need his stinking money, Victoria." He swallowed. "Why don't you start by telling me what happened in there before you start accusing me of stuff?"

"I thought you cared about me. Why would you set me up like that?"

"I do care about you, Victoria. More than you could ever imagine. I thought I was doing something right," he said in a voice that was exasperated.

"Right for you." I chuckled sarcastically. "When were you going to tell me you had taken on my father's case to countersue my mother?" I said. As the words came out, I couldn't believe how absurd it sounded. I couldn't believe how crazy my family was. "That's what Francis was trying to tell me that day, right?"

Jack went paler than his white oxford shirt. "I was going to tell you—"

"When? After George paid me off? After I got my mother to drop the lawsuit? You guys conspired to get this done."

"What? No."

"Isn't that what this is about? You wanted me to come with you to Vermont, so you and my father could use me to get what you guys wanted? I'm just a pawn in your game, and I went against my better judgment to be here with you." I rubbed my eyes.

"Wait a minute, that's not true! I was under the impression that he wanted to come here because he wanted you back in his life. I had no idea he was going to do that," Jack implored.

It was too late. Whatever he was telling me now would never reverse the damage that'd already been done.

"I hope I never see you again, Jack."

"You don't mean that."

"Oh, yes, I do." I nodded, making my way past him.

"Can you come back? Victoria!" he called out after me as I made my way to the cab.

"I'm sorry, Jack. I'm sorry you were robbed of any chance to make things right with your son, but it didn't give you the right to meddle in my life," I said, turning away to get in the cab and leaving Jack standing there, alone.

20

JACK

AS I ENTERED THE ROOM, my eyes took in the different types of whisky displayed on the walls throughout the Volary bar. This was the hard part because the urge to drink was still there. I knew if I ordered a glass of whisky there would be no limit to how much I would consume— but that was the past; today I was a different man. I spotted Greg, my longtime friend, sitting at a table in the back. He was a dating columnist for a popular magazine in New York called *The Avant-Garde,* and now with the launch of a new magazine, I didn't get to see him as often, but we still made time for each other, like today for lunch. I told myself before coming here that I would only have sparkling water with lime and the overpriced hamburger— and that was what I would do. I had thought about canceling my membership at this elite gentlemen's club, but then I enjoyed coming here for the food and the panoramic view of the Manhattan skyline. I guess as long as I realized my issues with alcohol and why I had this need for it—filling the void—then I felt like I was in control. Now more than ever I was determined to stay sober, especially since Victoria came into my life. She made me realize I wanted something more, something better, but then I blew it.

It hurt not having Victoria in my life anymore, but this time around, I wouldn't use a bottle of Macallan to numb the pain. I needed to feel it, and the only way was through abstinence.

It had been three months, *three whole months*, and I hadn't gotten a text or a phone call from Victoria. It ripped me apart. Victoria was upset and had every right to be, but I promised my intentions had been in the right place. When George Fairfax came into my office, I thought I could manipulate Victoria to convince her mother to drop the lawsuit. But, as I got to know Victoria and her past, I just didn't have the heart to do that to her ... because I cared for her more than I cared about myself—or my career.

Then, I had another smart-ass idea, the kind that would only bring a father and daughter back together. I'd genuinely wanted her to get to know her father and maybe make amends before it was too late—like it was for me.

I only wanted her to be happy.

"Hey, Jack." Greg's deep blue eyes acknowledged me as I sat in the cow-print club chair across from him.

"Where did you get that suit?" I smirked.

Greg's style had always been sharp, usually going for the classic look rather than chasing trends. So it surprised me that Greg showed up dressed in what appeared to be a size too small grey wool-blend suit with a crisp white shirt. Something was off.

"Are you making fun of me?"

"It's a little snug." I lifted an eyebrow.

"It's the latest trend," Greg said, adjusting the sleeve of his jacket.

"Is that what your tailor told you? You look like a Popsicle stick." I grinned, pushing the menu aside, knowing already what I was going to order.

"Staci said I looked sexy in this suit," Greg beamed.

That's what it was; he was trying to impress a girl. I thought I noticed a shift in Greg lately. When we went out, he seemed not to occupy himself with the attractive women in our midst.

He was infatuated with Staci.

"Right. I think she's just being nice," I smirked. "What's the deal with Staci anyway?"

For a moment, Greg did nothing but stare at me. "There is no deal with Staci. She's just someone I work with, and we spend a lot of time together because we're trying to get the magazine off the ground."

"Oh, that's why you can't stop talking about her." I flashed him a knowing grin. "So, when am I going to meet her?"

The waiter came to our table and took our orders. I was proud of myself for sticking to the plan, ordering the ground sirloin beef burger with bacon and cheese. Greg followed my lead and ordered a non-alcoholic beverage with his meal—a non-verbal gesture, but I knew he was supporting me.

"I'll admit I'm attracted to her, but I don't think she feels the same way," Greg said.

"Maybe she'll surprise you. You should tell her how you feel."

"You should come and write for us," Greg said, jokingly.

"Yeah, maybe," I chuckled. "Or maybe I should take my own advice," I said, rubbing the back of my neck.

Greg studied me before saying, "From the look of you, I take it you haven't spoken to Victoria."

Before I could reply, the waiter came back with our beverages, placing on the table a glass of sparkling water for me and a Coke for Greg.

"Victoria has my number. If she wants to talk, she'll call me," I said, before lifting my glass to my lips.

"Don't hold your breath," Greg mumbled. "Look, women can

hold on to grudges for years, maybe decades. A pencil you stole from her in elementary school or you mispronounced her dog's name. It's a talent, they have to stick it to you. You need to nip it in the bud before the wine ferments into vinegar."

It might be too late, I thought.

When our food arrived, I wasted no time in grabbing my burger and taking a bite before returning my gaze to Greg.

"One thing for sure, she'll forgive you faster if you tell her your side of the story," Greg said.

He was right. Victoria and I had unfinished business. She left my life abruptly before I could explain, and I probably hurt her more by not reaching out to her.

My gut tightened.

"It's been three months," I said.

"So what—better late than never. You're stubborn, you know that?" Greg let out a long breath before saying, "If you want Victoria back, you need to show her you're sorry. Regret everything that happened."

"I didn't really do anything wrong," I replied, but when the words came out of my mouth, I knew I was in deep denial.

Greg grimaced. "Do you really believe that? You betrayed her trust. Her father's an asshole and just wanted to reconnect to get something from her. No offense but I don't blame her for being upset with you. "

For a moment I forgot I told Greg what happened back in Vermont, but he's the only friend I could really talk to about this kind of stuff.

"I didn't know he was going to use her like a pawn, or else I would never have set it up," I said honestly.

"I know you had the best intentions, but you screwed up. Own it. Even the best of us do," Greg pointed out.

"Thanks, I feel much better now," I said, returning my attention back to my food.

"I know the real reason why you're not calling her," Greg said.

"Yeah, why?" I frowned.

"I see it with my readers. The majority of men tell me they feel relieved when the woman is the one to end the relationship, even though they don't want the relationship to end."

"That makes no sense."

"No, it doesn't. Your ego is getting in the way—making you believe that a good thing can't happen to you. I think a part of you is relieved that Victoria left you in Vermont because you feel like you don't deserve her."

My lips compressed into a flat line.

"I can tell you're in love—more than you've ever been. So let go of your ego. Stop being afraid that you might not be enough for her because you are." Greg lifted the white napkin from his lap and wiped his mouth with it.

"How do I do that?" I said, clearing my throat.

"Feeling secure in who you are—that's how. You have a good life—a good relationship with yourself. You don't need Colleen or Victoria or anyone else . . . that gravity that centers you has to be you. It's about time you realized that that's what Luke would have wanted for you. You deserve to be happy; the quicker you realize that, the faster the things you want in your life will come together," Greg said.

And as I sat there eating my lunch, listening to Greg preach, the only thing I wanted right now was Victoria.

"JACK!"

My whole body shuddered. I swore, she was going to give me a heart attack one of these days.

"What is it?" My eyes met with Helen, and I wondered how long she had been standing there at my office door, watching me stare blankly at my screen ... thinking about what Greg said.

I thought about Victoria.

"Helen, I have to prepare for my case. Just tell me what you want." My eyes shifted back to my screen.

What the heck did I type here? Instead of typing Ed Erickson, I'd written Victoria Fairfax. *What the hell is going on with me?*

"What's gotten into you? Didn't you hear me talking? I have never seen you like this since—"

"You don't need to say it," I cut her off, knowing what she was going to say—since Luke had died.

There was no pain in the world that could compare to losing a son, and Victoria was just another woman that I didn't need in my life, but why did it feel so bad?

These days, it was like I'd been walking in a fog. It served me right. That was what you got for caring, letting somebody in. It was only a matter of time before they shut you out. There was only one person you should care about—yourself. From now on, I would only put myself first, and last—like I had done before Victoria came walking into my life and brought the walls crashing down around me.

"You miss her," she said, and something in her eyes came across as sorrowful.

Great.

"Who?"

Helen was the last person I wanted to talk about Victoria to. I had to make Victoria a distant memory if I wanted to move on. Or at least, that was how I was going to play it.

"Shut up, Jack, and stop acting stupid. It's very unbecoming of you." She sat in the chair in front of me, her legs crossed, her back straight.

"I'm not acting anything. I'm annoyed at the interruption," I said, loosening my tie.

My hands went back to the keyboard. I felt her eyes burning into me, but I didn't dare to acknowledge her. Maybe she would get the hint and go away.

"The thing that amazes me is how you really believe that you're like this talented actor, strutting in here like everything is divine and great when, inside, you've been struggling with something big." She hesitated before saying, "You don't have to go through this alone. I am your friend, Jack."

"Aww, that's sweet, Helen. It sounds like you care about me." I grinned, knowing she was like me. We didn't do well with emotional stuff.

"I do care, Jack. You're the only one at this firm who wanted to take me on," she said.

"You're sharp and witty. Why wouldn't I? And, besides, your husband is the managing partner at my firm. It's not like I had a choice," I lied. I had known that I had to scoop Helen up before anyone did. She was the best executive assistant any man could ask for.

"Thank you for the compliment, but I know what you're doing." She fluffed her hair. "I have to admit, when Victoria came along and you guys got closer, I didn't think she would be good for you."

"Why not?" I said in a tone that almost sounded like I was offended.

"Because, Jack, you always get involved with women who only want one thing from you."

"My body." I smirked.

"Your money," she corrected. "Please, Jack, you have got to get over it. Without your reputation and wealth, you're really nothing special," she said casually.

"Thank you for flattening my ego and keeping me grounded."

"Well, someone's got to do it around here," she said. "But Victoria is not really like that."

"How would you know? You never met her—" I frowned.

But she talked over me, "Then, you stopped drinking, and it seemed like something had shifted with you. You seemed ..."

"Annoyed." I snorted out a chuckle.

"Happy." Her eyes met mine, and the air exited my lungs.
Could she be right?

"Wait a minute, how do you know so much? I don't think I ever spoke about Victoria. How do you even know her name?"

She shrugged. "The walls are thin, Jack."

"You mean, you've been eavesdropping?" I asked.

She gasped. "How dare you accuse me of such things." She flipped her hair. "Really, Jack, you're missing the point."

"Yes, please, let's get to the point," I said, leaning back into my chair.

"Call her, you big dumb oak!"

"Which one? Because I have a whole line of women waiting for my call." I smirked, but the look on her face told me she wasn't in a joking mood.

Honestly, I hadn't been with anyone since Victoria, and I was well aware of the reality that, when you had gold, no pennies would ever do. She'd ruined it for anyone else.

She was the only one who could flip the switch.

"I'm not going to beg a woman to go out with me. If she wants to see me, she knows where I am."

"Are you sure that's how you want to play this?" She tilted her head to the side.

I nodded. "Chasing after a woman who's not interested in you only makes you look desperate and pathetic."

"And weak?" she added.

"Exactly! No woman would respect a man like that, and I wouldn't want someone like that in my life."

And I was a man who wanted to be respected. But I hadn't respected Victoria's wishes, which I would have known if I had told her the truth. Maybe I should have had the conversation with her. It was true; I had been selfish. In the back of my mind, I had known I would benefit from Victoria and her father patching their relationship. I had merely set my ducks in line and allowed things to go organically. Maybe she could convince her mother to back down and turn over whatever evidence she had on the old man. That way, I wouldn't have to take on a case that I knew would be very possible for me to lose.

I hated losing, and now, Victoria was gone.

The irony of things.

What was I thinking, listening to George?

He'd made me believe he wanted to be a part of his daughter's life. I, of all people, could understand that. I was usually good at spotting snakes in the bushes, but Victoria had made me soft, and that had caused me to take my eyes off the ball. If I wasn't so consumed with regret in my own mistakes with Luke, I would have minded my own business, and I'd still be with Victoria.

I wondered what she was doing now. *Had she met someone else?* My heart compressed into a tiny little ball.

"She'll call when she's ready," I said sharply.

"Do you really believe that?" Her red lips tugged to the side. She knew something.

"They always do." I shot her a grin. "And, if she doesn't, then she doesn't. I'm not going to cry over it."

She stared at me.

"What?" I asked.

"For a man who's highly intelligent, you can be pretty stupid sometimes."

"Helen, do you speak to your husband like that?" I chuckled.

"When it's needed, yes," she said, her eyes fixed on me. "I

guess I was wrong. You never really cared about her or else you would stop making excuses and find a way to make things right between you two."

"And how would I do that?" I frowned.

"Start by apologizing, you big lump."

Why did I keep her around? Oh, right. She was married to one of the partners.

"How do you know I have something to apologize for?" I huffed.

"You think I don't realize, but you act like a jerk when you need to hide the pain you're feeling." She took off her glasses and wiped them with the end of her Chanel jacket.

"Helen, please, the next time I need help with my love life, I'll let you know." I shot her a look. "Can we get back to work?"

"Okay, boss." She got up abruptly and walked towards the door. "I know it's hard to trust someone after getting your heart broken, but do you think Victoria should be punished for something Colleen did to you all those years ago?" she said over her shoulder.

Her words reignited something within me. Man, this woman knew everything. Wasn't anything sacred around here?

"*Oh*, before I forget, those roses that were sent to apartment 204 on Corner Street were returned."

My head snapped up. That was Victoria's address.

"I didn't send any flowers." I furrowed my brows at her.

"Don't you remember, on Monday, after your meeting with your client?" She placed her hand on her hip. "You asked me to type out the deal points and send the most expensive red roses to Victoria Fairfax." She smiled.

This woman was relentless.

"I never asked you to send flowers."

"Really? I was so sure you did. My bad." She shrugged. "Anyhow, it seems that Victoria no longer lives at that address."

What?

My eyes pegged her at the doorway "She moved?" I asked, wondering if something had happened between Victoria and Scarlett.

"Yes, out of the country in fact." Helen turned and headed out of my office.

"Wait right there," I ordered, pulling away from my desk and walking over to her. "What do you mean, out of the country?"

"Apparently, she's been living in France for the last two months," she said casually.

"What? How?" I murmured.

"Do I really have to give you the logistics of it or—"

"Cut to the chase, Helen."

"Well, she's in some culinary course. That's what her friend Scarlett said over the phone."

"You spoke to Scarlett?"

"Interesting woman." Helen looked down at her freshly manicured nails.

"How long?"

"Indefinitely," she spat out.

A pain shot through my heart. *How could she just leave without saying good-bye?* I always thought this would eventually blow over, and Victoria would come back to me. I marched back to my desk and slumped in my chair.

How will I ever find her?

I looked up, and Helen was gone.

"Helen," I called out as I got up again, making my way across the office.

She appeared in the doorway, dragging a black carry-on with wheels behind her.

"What's that?"

"Your suitcase," she replied.

"Can you—"

"I cleared your schedule, and I took the liberty of contacting Anna, your housekeeper, to pack enough clothing for three days."

"Why three days?" I frowned.

"That's enough time for you to win her back."

"But I need my—"

"Here is your passport." She grabbed my wrist and placed it in my hand. "Victoria's address is written on a Post-it note inside your passport. A driver is outside, ready to take you to the airport."

"Helen, I—"

"You're welcome." She smiled.

"What would I do without you?"

"I don't know. What would Batman do without Alfred?" she said, and I chuckled.

I looked back at my desk, and it hit me. "How long has the intercom been on?" I asked Helen.

"Since I started three years ago," she replied. "It's not my fault you don't know how to shut the thing off. You can't expect me to do everything around here," she huffed. "But what are you doing standing there? Go now!"

21

VICTORIA

I HAD SPENT my Saturday afternoon alone, roaming around the city, and then I settled inside a café like I was one of the locals. I watched people through the café window as they walked on by on Rue Cler. This street was one of the most authentic market streets in Paris. With its cobblestone and tiny local shops, it had the charms of a little village. I could picture myself living here forever.

When I finished my coffee, I went next door to the *boulangerie* to buy fresh bread and then headed toward the little sleek *fromage* shop across the street that had a display of a variety of cheeses on pedestals under the bell jar. I had the urge to make goat cheese salad—a dish I'd learned last week, taught by my culinary teacher Pierre-François inside a retro-decor kitchen. It was interesting to have a classroom at the back of a candy shop with the black-and-white flooring and dark seafoam-green walls. I enjoyed the experience of learning new recipes, a new culture, language, and also meeting new people. However, something was missing, and I hated to admit it, but it was Jack.

There were so many times I'd wanted to pick up the phone

and call him, but what would be the point? He had been using me the whole entire time. I felt like I was used as leverage by Jack and my father, a way to get my mother to drop the lawsuit, but I hadn't spoken to my mother in months. The last time was shortly after I'd left Vermont. It seemed to me there were a lot of things she'd been hiding from me, too. I was tired of being lied to by everyone.

So, it'd solidified my decision to come to Paris. It was nice—this solitude. After all, this was what I wanted. I had come to Paris not only to learn French cuisine, but I'd also come because I needed a break from my life. I had been so busy with helping others and working hard to achieve my dreams that I had neglected myself ... and maybe I had come to forget about Jack, too.

I hadn't seen Jack since I left him in the parking lot. I was disappointed that he hadn't tried to contact me. I guessed I never really mattered to him to begin with. Anyway, it was for the best. It wouldn't have worked out between us. Luke had been our connection, and that alone would have never been enough to support a relationship.

As I walked out of the *fromagerie* and onto the cobblestone street, holding a couple of plastic bags containing items for tonight's dinner, I thought about Scarlett. We'd always had supper together. Even though I missed her, I realized that our time apart had done me some good. I needed something else, and maybe living together wasn't the best thing for our relationship. When I got back home, I knew I would be looking for another apartment. In the meantime, I was renting out a small one-room flat—literally a room with a bed in the corner, a small fridge and stove on the other side of the wall, and my bathroom inside a closet. But I didn't care. I was a New Yorker. I coped better in tight spaces.

I turned the corner and made my way on my street when my

eyes landed on something ahead. In the distance, there was a man standing near the entrance to my apartment building. He had his back toward me, dressed in a navy coat with the collar up. I wouldn't have given it a second thought, but from behind, he looked like...

Jack? My heart stopped for a moment. *It couldn't be.*

As I got closer, he turned and smiled, and the air from my lungs rushed out of me.

"Hey."

"Jack, what are you doing here?" I asked.

"I was in the neighborhood."

"In Paris?" I smiled, trying to compose myself. "Are you stalking me now?"

I allowed myself to believe he was here for me, but how did he know where to find me?

"I needed to see you." He stared into my eyes for several minutes before he said, "I have dinner." He lifted up the bag to show me, but his eyes trailed to my hand, and he realized we might have crossed paths on Rue Cler without even knowing it.

"Did you have any plans?"

"I do now." I smiled.

"ARE you sure you don't want me to help you?"

I sat at the small table. It was big enough to use as an accent rather than a dinner table, but it had come with the place. I watched Jack prepare us dinner. He was a man who was built to take up space, and standing in front of my two-by-eight kitchen, he made it look even smaller.

"No, I got it. I don't think I've ever cooked for you before," he pointed out.

"You haven't," I said like an afterthought.

There were many things we hadn't gotten a chance to do together. Maybe it was my fault, maybe it was his, but he was here now.

But why?

"So, what do you think about my place?" I asked, knowing his was a thousand times bigger.

"It's cozy and really clean." His eyes scanned the room before meeting mine with a grin.

"I know!" I laughed.

Jack had only been at my apartment in New York a handful of times since we dated—if I could call it that.

"Now, I know for sure the chaotic mess was because of Scarlett."

"Poor Scar. Her ears must be ringing," I said.

We hadn't talked about the last time we'd seen each other. *Why was he acting like nothing had happened between us?*

"Can I get you something to drink?" I asked, pouring a rich burgundy liquid into a glass.

"No wine for me," he said.

"You're keeping it up? That's great, Jack. I'm really proud of you."

"Why do you sound surprised? I haven't touched alcohol since you came into my life. You're so good for me. I was an idiot to let you go," he said.

My blood rushed through me, allowing the heat to wash over my body like a wave. *Had he missed me or thought about me this whole time apart, like I had with him?*

"You didn't let me go, Jack. We let each other go," I said.

He looked at me for a moment before turning back to the stove. "I, um ... I owe you an apology," he said, lowering the heat of the gas stove before turning to face me.

"Us being apart gave me time to reflect." He slid his hands into the pockets of his light, faded jeans. "And I realized that, back in Vermont, I put you in a spot that made you feel uncomfortable. I shouldn't have done that, and I'm sorry."

His face said it all. I could tell he regretted it. Maybe I was wrong. Maybe he had done it for my good, looking out for my best interest.

Because he cared? Because he loved me?

"After that day, I dropped your father as my client. It was something I should have done from the beginning because it wasn't worth losing you."

I sighed. "I *am* sorry. I walked away when I should have given you the chance to explain," I said, placing my wineglass on the table and glancing up at him.

"And you're giving me a chance now?" he asked.

Jack had a way of just looking at me that went through to the core. It was like I could feel and hear his thoughts, and it moved me. But I wasn't sure if I was ready to open myself to him, to allow him in again. *What if I was wrong? What if he broke me another time?*

"I have no choice. You're holding my dinner hostage." I smiled, casting a glance at the stove.

"I'm trying to be more—"

"Vulnerable?" I added, hiking my eyebrows.

"Don't push it." His eyes flashed a glimmer of amusement. "Jack Turner is never vulnerable."

Unless it was with me. I felt that in his eyes.

"Right. Jack Turner is a hotshot Tin Man." I laughed softly.

"I'm glad you find this amusing. You know I don't do emotions. It's not easy for me."

"I know, Jack," I said, allowing a serious tone to appear in my voice.

He pushed himself off the counter and straightened his spine. "Look, Victoria, I really wanted you to have what I'd missed out with Luke. I would have given anything for that kind of chance.

And, when your father had come to me, I genuinely thought he wanted to make up for lost time. And, if I'd thought for a damn minute that he would hurt you, I would never have allowed him to get near you. I will never let anything happen to you, let anyone hurt you—again."

What's that smell? My heart on fire?

"Oh, Jack, the food." I jumped off my seat.

He quickly lifted the skillet off the flames. "That was a close one." He chuckled. "I hope you like it slightly burned."

As I watched Jack maneuver himself in my Barbie-sized kitchen, I couldn't help falling into this—Jack, me, in Paris. It seemed so romantic. It was taking everything in me not to throw myself at him. But I didn't because things couldn't be rushed. He still hadn't made it clear what he wanted from me, from us.

"All right, here we go. I hope you like it." He slid the plate in front of me.

"What is it?" I looked up in amusement.

"I call it the Turner omelet." He sat in the chair in front of me.

"So, how long are you thinking of staying in Paris?" He cleared his throat before saying, "Indefinitely?"

I snorted a laugh. I felt like he was watching my every movement.

"It would be a dream, but unfortunately, I'm limited on funds, and my culinary course only runs for another twelve weeks," I said.

A look of relief came over his face.

"Well played, Helen," he murmured under his breath.

"What?"

"Nothing. It's just my secretary—it's not important. I thought you'd left for good."

"Scarlett told you that? Is that why you're here?" I frowned, wondering if he was scared that he was losing me for good.

I knew Jack wasn't a man who easily expressed his emotions, but I needed more from him, and if he wanted me in his life, then he had to prove to me that my time with him would be worth taking the chance—worth it even though my heart could get broken more than it already had.

"No, I didn't speak to Scarlett."

Everything went quiet until I said, "You know what's missing?" I pointed to my food with my fork. "The salt."

"I didn't put enough?"

He frowned, and I shook my head. As I got up to get the salt-shaker from the counter, he took my hand and pulled me closer.

"I've missed you."

When he looked at me like that, how could I resist kissing him?

But I didn't.

"Why are you here, Jack?"

"You know why," he said, tilting his head up so that he could meet my eyes. "I need you to know that, the time we shared, it mattered to me. I love you, and I miss you so much. Just tell me what I have to do to get you back in my life."

"I thought you didn't do the whole emotional thing." I smiled.

"I never told you that. Truthfully have so much to say," he said over my lips.

"I love you, too, and you don't have to say anything, Jack. I'd rather you showed me instead."

22

JACK

THE MORNING LIGHT came trickling in through the semi-sheer white curtains that covered the French glass doors in Victoria's bedroom. As I lay in the bed, naked, with Victoria in my arms, I realized I had everything I ever needed right here. No cars, no amount of money could ever make me feel more fulfilled than this moment right now.

I have Victoria, and she had me.

After Colleen, I'd thought love could only bring so much pain. I had sworn to myself I would never fall again, but this wasn't like before. This wasn't falling but rather coming into something, into a life I'd always dreamed of, but felt it was out of my reach.

Victoria's eyes fluttered open, and she propped her chin on her hand. Her eyes roamed over me, like I was basking in the sweet sunshine.

I leaned over and kissed her before saying, "Good morning."

She smiled, her silky brown hair spilled all around her. "Good morning."

Victoria was the sexiest thing I ever saw, and she was mine, at least for one more day.

"It's going to be hard to leave you tomorrow when I have to go back to New York," I said.

"I don't want you to go, but I understand," she said, softly nuzzling into my neck.

"What if I—stayed?" I asked.

"What?" she giggled.

"Yeah, we could live right here." I wrapped my arms around her.

"What about your firm?"

"I'll partner up with another one."

"And your cars?" she batted her lashes.

"I'll get a container and ship them over," I said, brushing a strand of hair from her beautiful face. "Then again, who cares about the cars. I have you, then it's more than I need."

The corner of her mouth lifted. "Jack, that's a good dream, but—"

"Let's think about it. We'll make a fresh start, and you can even open your catering company right here in Paris."

"You would do that for me? Leave everything you worked so hard for in New York?"

"Anything for you," I said, looking into her eyes.

"Wow, who are you?" she giggled. "And what did you do with my Jack?"

My Jack. I liked the sound of that. I wanted to be hers—forever.

"Why are you so surprise? Yeah, I have a hard time admitting my vulnerability. I've gotten better with age, but I still try to act as if I'm too tough to be weak. The truth is written all over my face, and I don't want to hide it from you anymore," I said. "I love you, Victoria, and life is too short to spend it alone. You're the only one who's found my soft spot. Now, I can't let you go." I grinned.

"What are you going to do, Jack? Tie me up?" She laughed.

I contemplated the idea for a brief moment until she poked me in the ribs, and I chuckled.

"I love you, Jack. I love the fact you're willing to uproot yourself for me but I'm coming back to New York in twelve months."

"I know but I don't think I could wait that long." I offered her a weak smile.

Helen knew how to use my fear of losing Victoria for good, to get me here. The whole plane ride to Paris all I thought about was if Victoria had moved on or worst—met someone else. I allowed my pride to get in the way because I was hurt that she shut me out. I never gave it a thought that maybe she was hurting too and that's why she hadn't reached out to me. Adults talked about their feelings, and maybe it's about time I grew up. It was clear to me now what I wanted, I needed to know she did too.

I glanced back at her. "Get dress. There is something I wanted to show you."

"Like what?" She smiled lazily.

"It's a surprise. I won't mess this up. Not this time." I gazed into her eyes. "It's my last full day in Paris with you and I want to make it memorable for us."

AFTER WE SPENT the morning having breakfast at a local café, we took a cab and made our way to the Louvre. The museum was crowded with people from all over the world, all walks of life. Everyone was here for a sole reason—taking time to appreciate the past. This museum was not only filled with artifacts and art, but it was also filled with evidence of someone's life

—heartaches and joys. These artists, sculptors—creators are no longer among the living, but they have left an impression on us—the way the world once thrived. Not many people have the privilege of leaving something monumental behind.

Then I thought of Luke. He might not have been an artist or a great sculptor, but he had still managed to leave an imprint on my heart.

He was still here inside of me. *Sometimes I forget that.*

I had worked so hard to build this life—this lifestyle. Money, cars, and women were all just a distraction because that was more entertaining than having to deal with myself—always feeling like I would never amount to anything. Then I had Luke, and I felt of all the mistakes I had made, my son was the only one I never regretted. For the first time in my life, I felt like I did something right. I had a purpose—to love a boy that would only know me as his godfather. After Luke died, I never thought I could be happy again, and it was easy to live without love because I felt I didn't deserve it. But now I had a second chance at love.

As Victoria and I made our way to the Egyptian antiquities, my eyes landed on a boy in the distance. There, by the Great Sphinx of Tanis, was a boy not much older than Luke was when I first brought him to the Louvre Museum. Headphones rested on his ears and an audio guide in the palm of his hands, and I couldn't help taking a minute to watch him as his eyes opened with amazement at the sphinx just like Luke's did. I held so much resentment toward myself and Colleen at how things had ended up, but at least she had granted me a week with Luke here in Paris. In my eyes, a week spent as a father and son. There at that moment, I wondered if I'd ever be a father again, but now with Victoria by my side, I was looking forward to the future.

Anything was possible.

We made our way from room to room, hand in hand, as we

browsed through some of the most famous paintings in the world, but the only masterpiece I saw was Victoria.

"What?" Victoria asked when she caught me staring at her. I took her into my arms and kissed her softly.

"You're the most beautiful woman I've ever seen," I said.

"I bet you say that to all the girls."

"No, because I never saw someone like you before. Your beauty is not only seen with the eyes but felt with the soul. My soul."

"Smooth." She smiled, wrapping her arms around my neck. "What do you want to do now?"

"There's a lot of things I want to do with you," I breathed into her neck. "But first, let's go eat. Then, I want to show you something," I said, rubbing her nose with mine.

WE ATE DINNER AT LOULOU, an Italian restaurant that had the most spectacular view of the Jardin des Tuileries, a 23-hectare garden located just behind the Louvre Museum. We were having a great time, and I didn't want it to end. As I watched Victoria's eyes light up when she talked about what she had learned in her culinary classes, and how passionate she was about it, I realized she was the one piece missing from my life. She was cute and sexy, and I liked who I was when I was around her.

After dinner, we stepped out into the garden as the sun faded in the distance, creating a magical autumn sky with various shades of pink and orange. My eyes brushed the sky, and I couldn't help feeling out of sorts because tomorrow I would be on a plane bound for New York without Victoria—at least for a few more months.

"So, what was it you wanted to show me?" she asked, wrapping her delicate hand around my bicep.

I smiled and pointed up at the Ferris wheel in the distance, lit up with millions of lights.

"You want to go on that?" She smiled and I nodded.

"I put Luke on that thing once."

Her eyes found mine. "I didn't know you came here with Luke."

"Yes, when he was four. At the time he was in remission ... I had hoped it was for good."

Victoria must have seen the sadness in my eyes because she halted in her step to wrap her arms around my waist, bringing me closer.

"He must have been so happy." She rested her chin on my chest and peered up at me.

"Yeah, he loved it. He said he felt like he was on top of the world," I said, my smile fading. "But it won't be there much longer."

"Why not?" Her eyes went from the big wheel, then back to me.

"I'm not sure why, but it won't be there this coming spring."

"That's too bad."

"But we have it tonight. You're not afraid of heights, are you?" I asked, bringing her collar up around her.

"No, not at all. Let's go," she replied. Taking hold of my hand, we made our way toward the big wheel.

A few short minutes later, we climbed into one of the gondolas, and I took my place next to Victoria. Within minutes, the metal doors shut, and it made its way up.

"It's so beautiful up here." Victoria was enchanted by the city lights, as I was by her.

I exhaled, a little nervous about what I would say next.

"What's the matter?" She placed her hand on my knee.

"You're not afraid of heights, are you?" A line appeared between her brows.

"Can I not look at you?"

"You can, but you're acting a little strange." She observed me closely.

"I just want to memorize everything about this moment." I brought her hand to my lips.

"Jack ... you make it sound like something bad is going to happen." She furrowed her brow.

"No, no more bad things." I smiled. "I thought I lost you, and I just want to live in the moment ... with you. I brought you up here because I wanted to continue the conversation we had this morning in bed," I began.

"About moving to Paris?"

"Well, if that's what it takes to keep you with me. I told you I couldn't let you go."

"And I wouldn't want you to." She tucked herself under my arm.

"That's what I like to hear." I kissed the top of her head.

"I'm glad I got to see the Mona Lisa with you," Victoria said.

"I'm happy I got the chance to be here in Paris with you," I replied. "But next time let's make our trip together longer."

"Well, you definitely took me by surprise. I didn't know you were coming," she said, and even though it was dark, I could tell she was smiling from her voice.

I didn't know either. But now that I was here there was only one thing I wanted to ask her, that was if I could stop shaking like a leaf.

"I came here with one intent."

"And what was that?" She pulled back to look at me.

I cleared my throat. "I need you ... I need you by my side, Victoria."

"But you do have me." She smiled.

"No, not like the way I want you ... marry me?"

I caught her gaze, and her smile faded.

"What?"

I pulled a teal-colored box from my coat pocket. It was the ring I purchased at Tiffany's before I arrived at her apartment. I was trying to find the right time to propose, but now here with the panoramic view of Paris all lit up at night seemed so magical.

"I know this might be too soon, but life is short and you're the one that I want." I opened the box to reveal an emerald-cut diamond engagement ring.

"Oh, Jack, it's beautiful," she said, as I pulled it out of the box and slid it on her finger before she could give me an answer. "It's a little big, but we can get it adjusted when you get back to New York," I said, watching her face mixed with bewilderment and joy.

"Our lives will never be perfect, Victoria, but I think we can find something in each other that we both want. You want a family, and I want to be a father again. Let's build our own legacy. Lots of kids, maybe a dog?"

"I thought you didn't like dogs." She smiled.

"A man can change. With you in my life, I feel like it has for the better."

"You're serious about this?" She turned in my arms to look me in the eyes.

"The ring is already on your finger. You can't say no— it's bad luck." I grinned. "I've never wanted anything more," I said, my eyes never leaving hers. "Say 'yes', Victoria."

She bit her bottom lip like she knew how to drive me wild. "Mrs. Victoria Turner ... I do like the sound of that." A smile appeared on her pink lips.

"Me, too." I leaned in and kissed her. "Is that a yes? Because if I can't have you, you will be the death of me." I stared into her eyes.

"Well, then, I can't let that happen." She smiled, running a hand along my chest. "Mrs. Turner it will have to be," she whispered before I deepened the kiss.

And as the wheel made its way up to the peak, I felt like I was on top of the world.

EPILOGUE

Victoria
Five Years Later

WHEN I REACHED the door of a three-story brownstone house, I searched for my keys at the bottom of my leather bag. I had been on my feet all day, and I couldn't wait to kick off my shoes and get out of these clothes. I pushed the door open with my hip and locked it behind me while balancing a paper box filled with sweets—leftovers that I'd brought back from my client's wedding. As I walked past the banister, I glanced up, catching the light on in the upstairs hallway.

"Hello?" I called out, but no one responded.

Maybe everyone was asleep.

I continued down the hall and into the kitchen. I opened the lights and placed the box on the kitchen counter, taking a moment to look at the logo—VT Events & Catering. After all the hard work and so many tears, I was finally living out my dream.

A month after I'd married Jack, it was an easy decision to take his name. The Fairfax name had never meant anything or had any meaning to me, and family was more than a name. It was home and surrounding yourself with the people you loved.

Jack was my home. My family.

I paused at the white banister and reached down to pull off my stilettos.

"Hello?" I called again as I made my way up the stairs.

The sounds of little giggles and shushing came out from Jane and Lily's room. They were hiding, and I smiled. They did this every time I finished late at an event. As I slid the door open, I saw the girls had made a tent in the corner of the room with the throw covers from the den. The space was in complete darkness, except the pink string lights that illuminated the girls' twin beds.

The closer I got, the louder the giggles got.

"Aha, I found you," I yelled, pulling the covers away to find the twins dressed in their light green pajamas, tucked in their father's arms.

Jack.

He beamed up at me. That sexy smile never got old.

"Mommy, you're home!"

They threw themselves into my embrace.

Best part of the day.

I looked down at Jack's content face. He was still lying on the bed of pillows, holding a children's book.

"How was your day?" he asked.

"Exhausting. I'm glad I'm home." I smiled.

Jack tossed the book aside and got up. "Okay, girls, bedtime."

They both groaned.

"Five more minutes, Daddy?" Lily said, tugging at Jack's sleeve.

"I already gave you five minutes," he said as he threw her over his shoulder.

She giggled even more. I tucked Jane into her bed next to Lily's.

"One more story!" Jane said.

"I've read *Goodnight, Moon* five times already." He planted a kiss on each of the girl's heads.

Jack was an amazing father. I thought about Luke often and how he would have been an amazing big brother. We had planned to tell the girls about their brother when they were old enough to understand. Luke would always be important to this family, and maybe he'd had a hand in me and Jack being together.

"Good night, girls." I blew out kisses.

Jack slid his hands in mine and pulled me into the hallway. Instinctively, my arms went around his neck, and Jack pulled me closer.

"What do you want to do now?" He smiled mischievously as his hands slid around my waist.

"Mmm ... want to watch something on Netflix?"

"Good plan," he chimed in.

"I'll get the popcorn," I said, pulling away, but Jack slowly brought me back to him.

He always brought me back.

"First, I want a kiss," he said, leaning into me.

As I looked into his eyes, I thought to myself, *damn, it's good to be home.*

MORE IN THE ONE LOVE SERIES

Two New York editors learn that their office feud and love-hate feelings could be the perfect way to find the love that they both have been looking for—that is, if they don't kill each other first.

Available on Amazon: https://amzn.to/2w7VW7r

THE PROVERBIAL MR.UNIVERSE

The Proverbial Mr.Universe

Olivia Montiano is moving forward—without her unfaithful and controlling fiancé and without her father's unrealistic standards that have ruled her choices for twenty-three years. Olivia can now make her own decisions about life and love. But when mysterious, handwritten letters appear, she's baffled—and influenced by their very personal nature.

Nick Montgomery's life hasn't gone as expected. He's a washed-up artist and has decided that he doesn't need romance—until he meets Olivia. The universe then intervenes in their lives, making their paths cross again and again. But Nick is hiding something that he thinks could affect their relationship.

Will the universe bring Nick and Olivia together? Or will the mysterious letters and Nick's own secrets keep them apart?

CHAPTER 1

Olivia had found an escape route on the far left, a red exit sign beckoning salvation but somehow she couldn't find the courage to venture out the door.

"Congratulations!" said an elderly woman, one Olivia didn't recognize.

"You look lovely. Are you having a good time, dear?"

"Thank you ... yes." She would have been, if the circumstances were different. If she weren't an absolute crazy mess.

Loud music and laughter circled around Olivia as she stood in the middle of the crowded room. Who were these people? They were too busy living their lavish lives to notice that hers was coming to an emotional standstill.

"Wow, some shindig you've got going on. I feel like I'm at the ... what's the name of that award show they do in Hollywood?" Paul asked, taking his place next to her.

"Are you talking about the Oscars?" She frowned.

And the Oscar goes to ... Olivia Montiano, for Sham of a Life. Too bad it had taken her five years to realize it.

Paul slightly nudged her arm, handing her a glass. "Are you all right?"

"Yeah, sure ... Why?"

"Well, you look a little pale." Paul playfully rested his hand on her forehead.

"Can you stop?" she laughed, slapping his hand away. "I'm fine."

Her brother Paul had always been handsome, tall and lean, but something was different about him these days. Maybe it was his light hair, freshly cut to a shorter length. Or maybe it was because he'd gotten his act together and now worked for their father.

"Yeah, I guess I'm a little overwhelmed." Olivia glanced down at her glass.

"Shit, do you even know these people?"

"Some," she said, smiling weakly. "It's overdone, right?" Olivia had had no part in any decision-making when it had come to planning her engagement party. Everything from the menu to the tablecloth was the work of Dario and the event planner.

"Well, your fiancé sure knows how to throw a party." Paul brought the glass to his lips but stopped midair. "Hey, isn't that the new mayor?"

Nodding, Olivia took a sip of her drink. "Geez, what is this?" She scrunched her nose.

"Whiskey." He chuckled. "Okay, drink up. It seems like you could use it."

Olivia wasn't much of a drinker—maybe a glass of red wine occasionally. Never in her life had she gotten drunk, because Dario thought it was immature. So Olivia had strived to be responsible ... maybe even a little boring.

Without hesitation she shot back the glass, wiping her mouth with the back of her hand.

"I didn't mean for you to chug it down. You're supposed to

sip it." Paul grinned, taking the monogrammed glass, with the initials *D&O*, from her hand.

She cast a glance over her shoulder and whispered. "Paul, do you have your cigarettes on you?"

"You don't smoke." His eyebrows gathered up.

"I'm an adult ... do you have one for me?"

"You're serious? I don't think it's a good idea."

"Come on. I feel like doing something destructive." Who was she kidding? She had never done anything bad in her life.

"I don't know what the big deal is. It's just a cigarette."

Paul peered around him, as if in deep thought. "All right, only this once."

"You're such a hypocrite."

"Do what I say, not what I do," he said, quoting their father.

Olivia rolled her eyes. "Where are you going?"

"I left them at coat check. I'll meet you outside in five."

She watched her brother make his way through the crowd. All night she had kept her composure: smiling, talking to her guests, even laughing at their not-so-funny jokes, never showing a clue about what was going on inside her. *Today is the day*, she told herself. She had reached the point of all she could bear. She needed to escape from this room, filled with people who believed social status and wealth were the only things that gave someone importance. At some point, she had been one of them, too.

Dario approached her from behind. "Olivia, come with me. I want you to meet Mr. Belanger."

"Who?"

"Come on. You know who he is." He cast her a look. "He owns half the commercial buildings downtown."

"Can it wait? I was—"

"Well, no. I don't want to keep him waiting." Catching his reflection in the glass window, he straightened his blue silk tie.

CHAPTER 1

He gave her a side glance. "I told you, you should have worn the blue dress. At least we would have matched tonight."

Who were they, Laverne and Shirley?

"I don't believe this shit. I've been trying to close this deal for weeks."

Dario had been irritating her throughout the night. And now, she was less than excited at the prospect of being paraded around the room like she was the show's main attraction. Her fiancé seemed to have missed the point of what should have been a joyous occasion. Instead, he had made it out to be something else entirely. Olivia wondered how she had allowed herself to get lost in someone else's life. Was there any hope of getting her own back?

She nervously spun her ring around, itching to take it off like a cheap wool sweater. This ridiculous, massive diamond ring would have made most women happy.

Not her.

Dario hadn't proposed the way she'd dreamed of; instead he'd brought up the subject of marriage like it was a proposition for a business deal. She knew he wasn't much of a romantic, but still ... When they were ready to take the next step in their relationship, she'd never have thought it would feel like a hostile takeover.

He quickly glanced at her. "God, Olivia, would it hurt you to smile?"

She closed her eyes, held on to her last breath, and walked away.

"Olivia?"

Turning the corner, she opened a door leading to the large terrace. As soon as it closed, there was an instant quiet and serenity. Only the faint sounds of cars and trucks heading east and west came from below. The Place Ville-Marie had the most spectacular panoramic view of the entire metropolis, and this was the reason Dario had wanted to have their engagement at the penthouse. She let her long red dress drag through the snow, walking closer to the end of the gallery.

The beacon light flashed across the sky, forcing her eyes back up, landing on the biggest star. She had a feeling that something was about to happen, something exceptional.

What would she wish for? Happiness? Love? A great career? Didn't she possess those things already? Most of her friends thought so. But Olivia knew the reality: when it came down to the fine print, it was a different story. These days the thread had been unraveling quicker than she could ever have imagined.

For several weeks, Olivia had struggled with the feeling she was not living the life intended for her. Olivia thought about Dario. Even if she had believed in soul mates to begin with, it was clear that Dario wasn't hers. Over time, Olivia had thought she could change him, but it turned out it had been Olivia who had done the changing instead. At first she had told herself that Dario only wanted the best for her.

Lies.

She had thought she could live with the fact Dario was a workaholic, like her father, and it didn't bother her.

More lies.

She had believed Dario was marrying her because he loved her, and not because of her father's wealth or connections.

More. More. Lies.

The truth had been in front of her all along, but she'd refused to see it for many reasons.

"Olivia? What are you doing out here?"

She turned around and found her sister Nina standing there, with the door half open. Her purple dress fit Nina like a glove. Her honey-colored hair, pinned up, gave her the allure of old-Hollywood glamour. Nina was four years older, but everyone said they looked alike. Olivia had never thought they resembled each other much, except that they both had inherited the same big caramel eyes from their mother. Growing up they had been close; all three siblings had their place in the family: Nina was a daddy's girl, and Paul was a mama's boy...and Olivia fell somewhere in between.

"Geez, it's cold." Nina brought her arms up, bracing herself for the winter chill.

"Where's Paul?"

Nina shrugged. "He said you wanted to do something destructive. What's that about?" She paused. "Are you crying?" Nina pulled her dress up, carefully walking closer.

"I can't do this."

"What?" Nina frowned.

"I can't go through with this charade ... I can't marry Dario." She covered her face with her hands.

Nina yanked Olivia into an embrace. "Hey ... Hey, it will be all right. Liv, seriously, stop! You will get mascara all over yourself, and me." Nina pulled back and reached into her purse. "I know what's going on..."

"You do?" Olivia took the tissue out of her sister's hand, wishing Nina could just read her mind.

"It's just cold feet."

Olivia's heart slumped. She knew it was more than that, but how was Nina to know? Olivia had been hiding everything from her family. There was so much they didn't know about her relationship with Dario.

"I had cold feet before I married Peter. It's only normal. It happens to some people."

"I don't believe you. You're just saying that to make me feel better."

"No, it's true. Ask him." Nina's teeth chattered.

"But Peter is good to you."

"Yeah, Liv. All men are brilliant in the beginning. They bring you flowers, sweep you off your feet, and when you marry them it becomes a different story." Nina brought her arms higher around herself, bouncing back and forth. "Suddenly you become this freaking 1950s housewife. Picking up his dirty socks at the end of the bed. Every. Freaking. Morning. Somehow they seem to forget what the laundry basket is for." Nina pulled a face.

"But you love him."

"Sure I do. We've been together for so long, but sometimes I wish we could go back to the beginning." Her smile faded. "Marriage is not a fairy tale, Olivia. Other things come into the picture. Mortgage, bills, kids—life has a way of sucking the romance right out of it. There are days I swear Peter gets on my nerves. I could just choke him ... But when I force myself to stop and think back to the first moment I saw him, and why I love him, it renews my faith in us." Nina's eyes softened.

"I don't know..." Olivia understood that relationships went through all kinds of changes. They evolved into something else, leaving a remnant of their former obsessive, passionate love behind. But if you didn't have the love to sustain the relationship, any snag could cause everything to unravel. She had heard this speech or something like it before, from Aunt Teresa to the sweet Chinese lady next door. It seemed everyone had a piece of advice since she'd gotten engaged.

Her dilemma was simple: what if she was making a terrible mistake by settling down before meeting the person she was supposed to love? Even at the beginning of her relationship with Dario, she couldn't have called it a great love story. Olivia wasn't sure what had sustained their relationship all this time. Perhaps it was love, but lately she had realized it had been her father. He was the one who'd set them up.

There was nothing more motivating than the fear of disappointing a parent.

Nina jumped at the sound of a crackling noise behind them.

"Ma, you scared the shit out of me." Nina placed her hand on her chest.

"Girls, I didn't think you were crazy enough to be out here. Quick, get inside! You're going to catch pneumonia." Their mother's voice came through the open glass door. She looked sophisticated in her shift dress and white pearls, the Jackie O. look. Even though their mother had arrived in Canada as a young girl, she had never managed to lose her Italian accent when she spoke English.

"We're coming, Ma." Nina shook even more. "What the hell are you made out of? Aren't you cold? Please tell me you're ready to go in."

Olivia nodded.

"Are you okay?"

Olivia took in a deep breath. "Yeah ... sure ... I'm just overwhelmed."

She spotted Dario from across the room, standing close to a very attractive blonde.

At what point had she forgotten that there were other choices?

LYRICAL LIGHTS

Lyrical Lights Mable Harper is a hard-working model trying to make her name in the fashion business. The only problem is that the world of fashion—and her agent—isn't really ready for a hard of hearing woman on a mission to challenge their patriarchal expectations. So after a string of unfortunate and unpleasant situations, Mable is relieved and glad her run of bad luck is over when a handsome, young stranger named Simon comes to her rescue at a bar. Then, when she runs into Simon once more before an unexpected opportunity revives her fashion career, she starts to wonder if it was more than a coincidence that she ran into this charming photographer.

As her modeling career flourishes so does her relationship with Simon—as he awakens desires she never imagined she had. However, as Mable falls more and more for Simon, she soon discovers there's more to him than wit and charm and his complicated past keeps coming between them.

Suddenly, Mable struggles to find a balance in her life in a world that keeps insisting on trying to tear her down, forcing her to choose between the life of fame that she always wanted and the man that, until now, she never knew she needed.

CHAPTER 1

Mable

The Little Orange House was the latest trendy bar in the Meat-packing District, a hot spot for the arts and fashion crowd. With an unfinished degree in computer science, I was still trying to figure out where I fit into the fold.

The bar itself was chic, a mix of Spanish and industrial revival. To my left, there was a concrete wall lit up by candles, each in their individual compartments. All the way in the back, past the iron gates, was where I sat alone on a rust-colored leather couch, away from the crowd and the rhythmic music that played on the speakers. Rather, I assumed it was music, because every-thing sounded like ruckus. I rarely liked to come out to these places; the commotion and the background noise would annoy the average person, but it could be very stressful for someone hard of hearing, like me.

I had been waiting here for an hour, and it was clear that Jason wasn't coming. But hey, I wanted to make it official. Besides, the martinis weren't half-bad.

CHAPTER 1

Jason?

How can I explain my relationship with Jason? I guess you could say it was in eternal purgatory—it fell anywhere between hooking up and something of a real relationship. A girl can get lonely in a big city with no other prospects in sight. You take what you can get. Besides, I didn't have time for a real relationship.

That's a lie; time was what I had in spades. I was a broke model, working part-time at an Italian deli on the Upper East Side. Technically, I wasn't allowed to work anywhere while under contract with the NY Model Agency. They literally had me on standby, waiting for the next job, but I hadn't heard a peep from my agent in over three weeks, and my debts were on the rise. With what I got from my dad and what Johnny paid me under the table, I managed to survive. Working at the deli wasn't my dream job, but the owners treated me well, especially the little one they called Nonna. She heckled me every time I got in her line of sight. *"Eata, eata ... you too skinny.* Don'ta worry, you make the model anyway."

I was damn fond of them, but holy cow, what was with these people and their obsession with food?

I only wished my agent Dania had the same philosophy. The last time we had spoken, she'd said, "Darling, you need to lose three more inches, okay? Around your waist and thighs." The sound of paper crackling came through the phone—what I assumed was my contract compressing into a nice little ball—and I swallowed. "That's if you want to work. If you don't, it's not going to happen, not here in New York City or anywhere else."

She was oblivious to the fact that I was two layers deep in my lasagna.

"I'm sorry, Mable, but it's not working out ... I have to let you out of your contract." She'd sighed. "I wish you luck."

It was business; if she didn't make money, then I couldn't pay my bills, and, unfortunately, I was the product she was selling. We weren't having any success with each other.

But the worst of it hadn't come from Dania—it had come from the designers themselves, who had related their concern that I wouldn't be the best match to represent their label, since I was hard of hearing. It caused me to talk funny.

I asked myself, constantly, why the hell I put myself through this. It was straightforward: the dream was bigger than me. It was like an entity of its own, making me believe that, if I held on a little longer, if I could prove to them that my disability was an asset, I could represent girls who were different. I thought things would happen, just maybe.

So tonight, I had hoped Jason would be able to console me, like I had many times for him. I should have known better. When a guy said, "I'm not looking for a serious relationship," it most likely translated to, "I have no intentions of having one with you —like, ever." But my mind was a tricky little gal, the kind to concoct a better truth, one that suited me better. I had failed miserably at conforming him to boyfriend material, but I couldn't blame the guy. He had laid it out for me, but did I deserve better? Sure, I did. But I had allowed this shit-show to run its course for several months because I believed it was better than being alone. With every passing minute living in this metropolis, my views on dating had reformed into something more cynical. After a while, you realize that everyone around you complains about dating in New York.

As soon as I finished my glass, I ordered another one. I thought, *I surely deserve it*. I had a plan. Tomorrow I would call my dad and tell him he was right, that this whole modeling thing was a waste of time. In a few weeks, I would return home to Montreal and continue my studies, like we'd agreed. But on the bright side, at least, after a year of putting my body through hell, I had been fortunate not to develop an eating disorder like some of my colleagues.

Within minutes, the waitress brought me an apple martini, and I reached over for my purse beside me. I swept my hand on the soft leather ... nothing. A surge of anger came over me.

"My purse was here just a minute ago, and now it's gone," I said, looking up at the twenty-something waitress, who looked like she couldn't be bothered. She repeated something, but I had no clue what Miss Muffet was saying. The music was blaring in the background, drowning the sound of her voice. All I could see was her bright pink lips flapping in the dark, but they were moving way too fast for me to catch anything. It's a misconception that a deaf or hard-of-hearing person can read lips—that we have developed a sixth sense to compensate for our disability. If that were true—I was still waiting for mine to kick in.

"Can you ask the bartender if anyone found a purple boho bag ... with a gold clip?" I was yelling at this point—I couldn't hear my own voice. She stood there, showing me my bill, and those damn lips still flapped.

"Yes, I would like to pay for my drinks, but someone took my purse ..." *This is crazy.* "I can't understand—I'm hard of hearing ... can you please write it on your phone?" I saw her smartphone peeking from the pocket of her black apron. Talk, talk, talk ... Her mouth kept going, and I was getting annoyed with her expressions. I was raised in the hearing world and had never deprived myself of anything any other twenty-one-year-old like me was doing. Never allowed my disability to impede anything.

Good grief, talk about an off night.

"Okay, just give me a second." Obviously I wasn't getting anywhere, and instead I focused on finding my bag. It was possible it could have fallen on the ground or gotten kicked under the couch. I got on all fours to look around, and that's when I stumbled across a pair of navy oxford shoes. I forced my eyes up the length of the muscular legs attached to them. Then a set of hands appeared, guiding me up, and I straightened my body.

When I did, my eyes met the most expressive, soft, ultramarine eyes I had ever seen. And I found myself speechless. I would have expected no one to come to my rescue, but there he was, with a laid-back vibe in his style. He'd come with a gorgeous smile and light tousled shoulder-length hair. Without a doubt, I knew I was in for some trouble.

"Are you all right?"

"Someone took my purse," I replied. I looked past him and realized Miss Muffet had disappeared.

"No worries. I took care of it." As he spoke, I looked at his face.

"Do you want to talk outside?" I pointed to my ear underneath my hair. He nodded, but I was aware he didn't grasp my situation. It was pointless to explain, but he would soon find out.

STAY IN TOUCH

Sign up for a monthly newsletter, Maria will share her writing updates, new releases, exclusive content. Plus giveaways!

Maling List

Join Maria La Serra's Facebook group:

Social Peeps

Find all Maria La Serra's books here:

AMAZON

iBOOK

NOOK

KOBO

ABOUT THE AUTHOR

Maria La Serra lives in Montreal. Before becoming a writer, she worked as a fashion designer. She will try everything at least once, except for skiing, hiking or camping- okay anything relating to activities done in the great outdoors. When she's not working on her next book, you could find spending time with family.

Connect with Maria!
www.maria-laserra.com
authormarialaserra@gmail.com

www.ingramcontent.com/pod-product-compliance
Lightning Source LLC
Chambersburg PA
CBHW031322170626
46807CB00002B/529